SNOOP
(A Small Town Gossip Mystery)

by

Lyla Fox

For information, email **Cozy Cat Press**, cozycatpress@aol.com or visit our website at: www.cozycatpress.com

COZY CAT
P R E S S

ISBN: 978-0-9881943-7-3
Printed in the United States of America

Cover design by Betsy Fox

1 2 3 4 5 6 7 8 9 10

Acknowledgements

To Betty, Blanche, Suzi, Carl, Judy, Maris, Kristen, Karen, "Dr. D.," Julie, Kim, Sheila, Mary Jane, Bobbie, David R., Sue, Dottie, and always Ginger, as well as the cast of hundreds more, who supported me, and, of course, forever appreciation to my mother, L. Frances Fiscus Overton, who read to me. Finally, boundless gratitude and love for their unswerving belief in me, to the loves of my life: Bill, Tate, and Betsy

Chapter One

My knees were shaking and my eyes were bleary by the time I arrived at the newspaper. To add to my already nerve-frazzling day, I was sure that to further aggravate my morning, my father, Harley "Scoop" Hayes, would be late. But surprise of all surprises, Scoop sat waiting for me in his last-of-the-rummage-sale style. I guess a bloodcurdling murder will get even the most committed reprobate out of bed and to the office.

"You doing ok?" He looked up from his desk with uncharacteristic concern.

"I'm fine." Thrown by his sudden fatherly attentiveness, I quickly went to the most critical topic. "Is that Elli's obituary?" As I said it, chills raced through me. Elli Lundy really was dead. She really had been murdered.

"I just finished it. You can look it over to give it your stamp of approval, if you want. There's only so much time I can spend on it before it turns my stomach." He took several gulps of coffee.

Deep down, very deep down, I knew my dad had a heart, but it took an incident as horrible as what had happened to Elli to remind me.

Like my father, I could only read so much before I had to lay the article aside. "How much are you putting in the paper? Are you going to tell the whole town how badly she was hacked up? It will scare everyone to death." Now I needed a strong cup of Scoop's very hot sludge.

"We're newspaper people, aren't we?" Scoop bristled. "It's our duty to keep the people apprised of what's going on down the street from where they live. We don't want to terrify them, but we need to plainly and simply tell them that this town isn't as safe as it was a few days ago."

"Right." I walked to my desk at the opposite corner of the room, turned on my computer screen, and tried to make some sense of what had happened in our Norman Rockwell little town only hours before.

For as long as I, Samuels Harper Hayes, could remember, my father has been a blessing and a curse in my life. Perhaps I had unwisely put the latter in the back of my mind when I decided to use a small portion of my gigantic trust fund to buy into *The Corner News*. It was a sound decision, I had told myself. Becoming part owner of my dad's rundown paper would also get me away from a mother with a penchant to control me, a stepfather pretty eager to see me go, and a boyfriend I could either marry or flee. Scoop and the paper had been my nice, safe escape hatch—until now.

"Look, I'd like to spill the beans and tell everyone the deadly details," Scoop stood next to me, "but I don't make the rules." He softened his tone as he gave his scraggly, gray ponytail a tug. "Trey was here just before you arrived. He told me, 'Ixnay on the urdermay'—that's pig Latin for nix on the murder. He doesn't want us to say anything until they have the killer behind bars or at least can give people enough information that they don't become paralyzed with fear."

"Trey Davis should talk. When did he ever keep his mouth shut! Ever since they made that jerk our police chief, there hasn't been a secret that hasn't leaked out of the police station."

"He's not the sharpest tool in the shed, I agree." Scoop pointed to the coffee pot, his signal that he wanted me to get him another cup. I shook my head. I'd been hired as his accounts manager and copy editor as well as his junior partner. There was no way I was his coffee maven.

"Aren't you a little concerned that the man in charge of finding a killer can't even find his way home after a late night at the bar?" I ignored Snoop's second signal to get him coffee.

"I doubt that the county sheriff's department will let Trey handle this by himself. He didn't go from being a termite inspector to police chief because he is a keen investigator. More likely, no one ever thought he'd have more to do than get a cat or two out of a tree." Scoop laughed at his joke, which wasn't nearly as funny as he seemed to think it was.

In truth, ever since Scoop won partial custody of me when I was in second grade, we've had a love/hate relationship. I loved him, for the most part, and my mother hated him, also for the most part. When I told her I was leaving my luxurious Chicago digs to move back to Cotter's Corner, she didn't speak to me for a week. If you knew my mother, you'd know her silence wasn't altogether a bad thing.

No matter how hard I tried, I couldn't forget about Elli and how rude I'd been to her the last time I saw her. I'd let her down. Usually I work to be kind to everyone, but I'd been pressed to meet deadlines when Elli stopped in. I knew she'd heave a ton of gossipy talk my way and I wouldn't get my work done.

Don't get me wrong, I absolutely love gossip in all forms from juicy items for my weekly column *Snooping*, to those articles in grocery store tabloids that cause me to clog the lines and have dirty looks shot my way. But yesterday morning when Elli showed up, I had dozens of bills to pay, copy to edit, and advertisements to create. In a day when print journalism is disappearing faster than New Year's resolutions, our paper has survived, even thrived, because we work hard to give the people of Cotter's Corner what they want— gobs of town-related, totally unimportant information. If I'd only taken the time to listen, I might have saved her life.

"Did Trey tell you whether or not they have any suspects?" I tried to push away the guilt I was feeling.

"No suspects. He's sure that it was random and someone from out of town. The general consensus is that Elli probably opened the door expecting to see a friend and was accosted by someone intending to rob her. Everything got out of hand pretty fast is my guess."

"I think Trey's wrong, that it's not as simple as that."

Scoop kept talking, but my mind reverted back to the last time I'd ever see Elli.

"Hi," I'd said without even taking the time to establish eye contact.

"I'm going to have big news for you in a day or so," her gravelly voice proudly announced.

"Good," I'd responded, still not looking up. That was all I'd said, "Good." *So wrong.*

"Big, big news." Looking back I see that she was desperate to convince me she had something worth listening to. "Hey, Sam, did you hear me? I said I have something really huge to tell you."

Her tone told me she was getting irritated so I stopped what I was doing to look up. "Tell me about this big news."

"I can't yet, sugar. But just you wait. In a day or so, I will waltz in here with information for the paper that will knock your socks off."

"Can't wait." I returned to checking my figures. Even then my words seemed flat and emotionless.

"Remember that I can't tell you for a few days, though." Her eyes begged for some indication of enthusiasm.

"Well, let me know as soon as you can tell me." I felt a rush of shame as I considered how patronizing my tone must have sounded. I'd been callous and discounting of someone who only wanted to help fill my gossip column.

But now Elli was getting a lot of attention, the kind everyone dreads. Over the next few hours, calls to the paper revealed how differently people were reacting to her murder. Some callers were eating it up, asking for more blow-by-blows regarding the elderly woman's violent death. Others asked—no pleaded—to hear that the perpetrator had been caught. Like me, they didn't want to think that their lives were as much in danger as Elli's had been.

For the first time since I'd moved to Cotter's Corner a year-and-a-half before, I seriously considered throwing all my things in bags and driving fast and furiously back to Chicago. My mother's posh home and state-of-the-art security system beckoned me. It was one of those times that I saw the advantage of being the stepdaughter of Leland Henry, Esq., billionaire and power broker. The irony of seeing Chicago, with its big city dangers, as safer than little, out-of-the-way Cotter's Corner was not lost on me.

I watched the people walking by the newspaper. Some hurried as though they worried that whoever killed Elli was after them, too. Others seemed oblivious to the ominous cloud hanging over the town. But I saw the change that Elli's murder brought, and I saw it quickly. The fear that embraced the town was palpable.

I bet she gave her murderer a good fight, I thought. Rumor was that Elli had been a hard-drinking, barroom brawler in her day, but gave it all up a decade or so ago when she found religion. Recently she'd restricted her activities to laying both wallpaper and an occasional beau from her Pentecostal church. "All in God's good graces," she'd say.

People echoed a version of the same sentiment when they heard about the murder in our one-horse, one-stoplight town: "Cotter's Corner is not a place where you'd expect to find anyone, let alone an old woman, strangled and bloodied." I certainly hadn't expected it. I'd moved from Chicago to get away from Yates Logan and the seamier side of life in a big city. Oh, and to get away from my job at the textbook publisher which had become boring and cutthroat. When the body of one of the women with whom I worked was found floating face down in the Des Plaines River, her throat slit, I no longer had trouble deciding whether or not to take my dad up on his offer of half the paper for some of Leland's generously doled out lucre. Life had graphically reminded me that you could be here one minute and floating down the river the next.

"Trey Davis isn't going to give up on the idea that Elli's murder was the result of a botched robbery," Scoop said as he set type. "His higher thinking skills are pretty low. Only he would look at that dump where Elli lived and think there was anything someone would want to steal. It doesn't make sense. Trey may be a dick but he is no Dick Tracy." He went back to work, and I returned to trying to keep my mind off Elli.

"Where are you going? Don't we have deadlines for getting the advertising in?" I asked an hour or so later when I noticed Scoop slithering toward the door.

"Hey, you may be part owner now, but I am still editor and publisher," he snapped defensively. "I'm only going to be gone an hour or so. I got a date."

Even a murder couldn't keep my geriatric Don Juan from his bad habits. Booze and women. Those two issues killed his marriage to my mother and also the two marriages before that.

"You should have seen him," my mother said during one of the few kind conversations we ever had regarding Scoop. "There he was the most talented reporter on the Free Press staff. I was a college intern so smitten with his keen mind and taut body that I totally missed the stench of booze and philandering."

That was the most generous my mother ever got about the man who got her pregnant when he was thirty five and she was twenty. Soon after they'd married to legitimize my birth, he'd been fired from his job with the Detroit paper and had put their paltry savings into the small Cotter's Corner paper. Mother stayed with the marriage for three years and then left, with me in tow, for Chicago and a bigger, more exciting life with a much richer but no more faithful husband.

After Scoop left to pursue his nefarious activities, I poured the last of the coffee, made another pot, and took a look at the columns and articles awaiting my editing skills. Today I simply couldn't focus. There was space for two more items in *Snooping* but the only topic of real interest I had to offer was Elli's murder, and Scoop had prohibited me from writing about it.

What if the murderer was one of those people walking by the newspaper or eating lunch down the street at Mabel's Restaurant? My goose pimples got goose pimples just thinking about it. What had Elli been going to tell me that was so awful someone might have been willing to kill her to keep her from talking?

"Sam?"

I nearly jumped out of my skin when I heard my name. When I saw who it was, I didn't calm down. Charley Cotter has always given me and every other woman within his radius steam heat.

"Wow," he pulled up a chair next to mine. "You look like you've seen a ghost." His bronze god good looks rendered me nearly speechless.

"I was just thinking about Elli Lundy."

"I know." Charley who is usually all charm and swagger seemed almost thrown off his game by the previous night's horrific doings.

"She was here yesterday, and I was too busy to talk to her," I confessed.

"Don't hold it against yourself." He fixed his cobalt blue eyes on me, and totally shook my concentration. "Elli was a talker. We've all done our share of trying to escape before she'd hold us hostage with some story she'd already told us ten times before."

"I know. But this time, I think she had something serious to tell me. That's what she said anyway."

"She always thought her stories were serious." He smiled his perfect smile. "Let yourself off the hook. Elli was being Elli."

"I guess. Trey thinks it was robbery."

"Probably. It happens in even the best of places."

I doubted that Charley just popped in to talk. He lived most of the time in Florida, but came to town a few times a year to visit his father and to attend various Cotter-connected board meetings.

"Is there something we can do for you?" I pretended to tidy my desk.

"Always, Sammie." He hadn't called me that in years. My engine revved as I recalled the exact time and place. "I'm moving back here to help dad at Cotter Manufacturing so I'm also bringing my restoration business here, too. I need to buy some ads from you."

"You have a business?" I didn't mean to sound so surprised, but to those of us who worshipped Charley Cotter from afar, he was a first-class playboy, a rich man's son who appeared to do little except travel widely and spend his father's money lavishly. That was the word on the street anyway.

"Sorry to disappoint, but I'm not the scoundrel I'm reported to be. I actually work for a living, or part of it anyway."

"I didn't mean to sound surprised, but you're not around much so I guess I assumed you played a lot of golf in Florida."

"Tennis," he corrected. "And I do, but I also restore vintage autos. It's something I've done since I graduated from college."

"You graduated?" Another surprise. The town gossip had him kicked out of half a dozen prep schools and as many colleges.

"I actually did graduate, Miss Hayes. Not first in my class like you probably did, but I managed a degree."

"I'm really messing this up, aren't I? I mean, you came in here to do business, but all I'm doing is insulting you."

"Elli's death has us all operating at an alternate speed," he smiled his heart-stopping smile. "You know, though, I do think you owe me a bit of an apology. How about dinner some night?"

I couldn't see or breathe. Since that summer when I was sixteen and Charley was in his first year of college, he had been my dream man. But in no way was my reality ready to take on the fantasy. My mother had messed up her life by falling for a love 'em and leave 'em guy. I had spent my adult life making sure I didn't follow her missteps. If Yates Logan had been nothing else, he'd been reliable.

"Right," I laughed, pretending that I thought he was kidding, which he probably had been.

"Yeah, right," he reined in his charm and stood up to leave. "Well, how about you draw up something pitching my business?" He reached into a pocket of his black leather jacket. "Here's a brochure and my business card." His smooth, elegantly manicured hand brushed mine as he handed me the card. "I'll be back in a day or so to see what you come up with."

He left and I had more regrets. Now I had Ellie *and* Charley to lament. He was hot and sexy and très eligible. If I hadn't been scared to death of his intoxicating charm and lady-killer reputation, I would have jumped on his comment about dinner. But I couldn't risk it. It had taken my mother years and half of my childhood to repair the damage that had been done by her marriage to Scoop. Charley was a mistake waiting to happen, as half the married women in town could probably attest.

I forced myself to get to work. My column *Snooping* started out as a kind of Lake Woebegone meets *Reminisce,* but it has taken on a flavor all its own lately, a combination of humor, tabloid journalism, and recipes. A syndicate has even approached me about an Internet blog. I've played around with a couple of things lately, but nothing concrete.

I mentally gave myself one last kick for letting Charley slip away and then jotted down a couple of ideas for a blog. When nothing substantial sprang to mind, I searched through my files for Elli's no-bake cheesecake and turtle-toffee cookie recipes. I'd reprint them both in homage to an old friend.

Living up to my low expectations, Snoop didn't return. I finished the draft of my column and gave myself permission to close up ten minutes early. I needed to get home to Messy.

It's a short walk to my house so I do it unless the weather is particularly fierce. Even though it was early November, it was warm and the leaves were still a full palette of autumn hues. Cotter's Corner is pure New England in Michigan. Its houses are rimmed with gingerbread and its trees stand lush with leaves. The walk home usually delights me, but today I felt uneasy. I made sure that no one was running toward me, hatchet in hand.

"Hey, there, Messy." My rescue pooch, found along I-94 on one of my trips to and from Chicago, raced toward me the minute I opened the door of my quaint Cape Cod. "I bet you want to go out, don't you?" I hugged my part-golden retriever, part-mystery hound and opened the back door to watch her race into the big, fenced-in backyard.

I left Messy happily chasing squirrels and went back inside to pour myself a glass of iced tea. Next, I fired up my laptop and sifted through my messages to see if there was anything urgent.

I next clicked onto *People* magazine to see what the rich and famous were doing. Predictably, someone had left her husband for her reality-show dance partner; someone was dating his much younger personal trainer, and someone had gone into a treatment center. After my gossip du jour, I went to several other favorite sites. My friends tease me that my lit degree from DePaul isn't well-served by my addiction to social media and yellow journalism. I get defensive because I know it's true, but someone got me into it when I was young, and I can't get out of it, nor do I want to.

The answering machine blinked three messages. I took them from worst to best. The worst was my mother's semi-weekly plea to move back to Chicago. I would put off returning her call, and when I did, I would give her my pat answer: "I may one day return to

Chicago, but that won't be soon." She wouldn't understand that as I neared thirty, cozy and quiet trumped lights, camera, and action.

The second message was from the tirelessly persistent Yates. I gave him points for believing that if he hung in there long enough, I would weaken and return to him and the engagement I'd broken just before I put the pedal to the metal and headed to Cotter's Corner. I confess, I did have second thoughts when he of the Clark Kent personality and Superman physique unexpectedly showed up at my little house and wooed me into bed with his demanding kisses and perfect body. Those moments, although pleasant, weren't memorable, and when he drove away, I always felt more relief than desire. In the last six months, he'd shown up only once. Perhaps my taking him to dinner and then offering him the guest bedroom finally convinced him that we were truly over.

Unfortunately, my mother has not given up on my reconciling with Yates. Every conversation I have with her ends, "I hope you give Yates a call. Leland says he still misses you." In our last conversation she threw in, "You know you might lose him. The girls in the office all drool over him." Good. I thought to myself, let them drool.

Yates is the perfect man to my mother, who would never sacrifice material wealth for love, not after my father anyway. "I learned long ago," she has said at least a hundred times, "that no matter how much you think you love someone, he can disappoint you. Money never will."

Leland has disappointed my mother, too. He had divorced his wife of thirty years to marry her, a much younger, prettier version. And now there are other younger, prettier versions. "But I know he'll never leave me. I'm the one he really loves," she told me after a particularly embarrassing scene at the country club when a woman young enough to be his daughter hopped onto Leland's lap and told him she loved him. "He's a rich man, a great catch," my mother said defensively as she jangled a new diamond-laden, apology bracelet worth enough to feed a small nation.

As far as I'm concerned, the best times with my mother were before Leland and after my father when she'd made all my clothes, gone to business college nights, and worked as a salesclerk during the day. When Leland offered her his power and security, I'm sure it was all my mother thought she ever wanted. But she's not happy. I know that every time I see her around my father. No matter how loudly she protests, I know that *he* was the love of her life.

"Don't make the same mistake I did," is all she says in reference to my father. I confess to a perpetual fear that a Scoop Hayes clone will come along to charm the pants off me and leave me barefoot and pregnant. Though Leland's trust has given me massive and permanent financial security, I still irrationally see myself left one day in the same dire straits in which Scoop left my mother.

Though my mother and I are in a nearly constant state of war, I have great empathy for the shy young college girl from an Ohio farming community whose pregnancy by a twice-married letch nearly destroyed her life.

I had definitely saved the best email for last. It was from my college roommate Rose. A Mormon from Utah, Rosie reads *The Book of Mormon* daily and sends me Mormon elders whenever she thinks I need them. As different as she and I are, I adore her. Since she graduated and went back home to Utah, she has been busy having children: four at last count. And though I think she's nuts to populate the earth in such a seemingly reckless way, I have to say her marriage and life appear rock solid. The best thing about Rose is that, unlike my mother, she has never voiced one word of criticism where I'm concerned. She visited Yates and me during my last year in Chicago and never mentioned our "living in sin." All she ever says about my love life is that one day she hopes I find the man of my dreams. Her phone call was to invite me to Utah for Christmas. I just might go. Leland and mother would be at their place in Hawaii, and my dad hates the sentimentality connected to the holidays. Once Elli's murder was solved, I would be Utah bound.

Before I left the computer, I checked Facebook one more time. I'm not a lover of FB because I'm not sure anyone is really interested in my pretty dull life, and most of the time, I'm not very concerned with their "waking up with a headache" or "having a bad day at work." Once in awhile an old friend might write something interesting, and that's the only reason I don't permanently deactivate.

I suddenly got the urge to see if Charley was on it. There it was. Cotter Restoration. All it had was Charley next to a variety of gorgeous autos in a variety of spots from Italy to France to Germany. It had been nice to fantasize about Charley when I knew there was little chance of seeing him. I'd better get my libido in check now that he was moving back.

I clicked off and went upstairs to change into sloppy, comfortable clothes—a raggedy tee-shirt and worn, ripped jeans. I pulled my shoulder length, chestnut-colored hair into a ponytail and wiped the day's grime off my face, glad that very little make up still did the trick. My mother had spent a small fortune in time and money to keep her face free from lines and her body small and perfect. I didn't need that yet, and when I did, I doubted I'd opt for a cosmetic "touch up." My face was my face and I liked it. However, I did miss Yates' saying, "You are a beautiful, sexy girl, Samuels." I loved hearing him say it, but also knew his adoration of me was tied as much to my being the boss's stepdaughter as to any passion he might or might not feel. Yates was a pragmatist if he was nothing else.

I went outside and threw Messy some balls. We both needed the exercise, but all of a sudden, in the middle of my own backyard, I felt uncomfortable, alone, and a little scared. One neighbor had left for her winter in Florida, and another, Mr. Smith, was a retired postal worker in the early stages of Alzheimer's. Not much help there either.

"You'd save me if someone came after me with an axe, wouldn't you, girl?" Messy galloped up with her treasured, blue racquet ball in her mouth. I realized that the only thing about Messy that might intimidate a homicidal maniac is her size. She's a fairly big dog. But if the dastardly intruder didn't run off immediately when he saw my lumbering hulk of canine mischief, I was a goner because Messy's next step is always to lie down in front of anyone willing to watch and show them her totally submissive, non-alpha personality. Up until now, I had loved that about her. At this particular moment, however, I considered adopting several pit bulls or a mastiff, who could intimidate the hell out of an intruder and drown him in their slobber.

The gate slammed and I jumped three feet. No worry. It was friend, not foe.

Agatha Chestnut, over forty years my senior and light years ahead of me in energy and spunk, raced toward me.

"There you are. I thought you might be at the paper so I went there first."

Dark smudges of something dotted her cheeks and chin. I tried to wipe a little away with my thumb.

"Don't bother," she gently brushed away my attempt to tidy her up. "It's ink. I was making a template for a quilt I'm designing. The pen exploded in my hand."

There was absolutely nothing I could say. And if I tried, I was afraid I would laugh.

"But," she stood straight and lowered her voice signaling she was about to make a dramatic announcement. "I didn't come to talk about me. You heard that Elli was murdered, right?" She brushed away a tear.

"I did."

"I can't believe my best friend is gone. My very best friend."

Again, I could add nothing except a hug. First, I never thought of Elli and Aggie as close. Most of the time they were locked in competition, either fighting over whose quilt was the prettiest, whose idea was the best, or whose brownies were the tastiest.

"When it hits so close to home, it really shakes you up, you know." Aggie leaned into me. We'd reversed positions since she was my summertime babysitter, providing comfort, treats, and her already-read *National Enquirers* and *People* magazines.

"They'll find out who killed her. I know they will. We'll have all the answers soon." I put my arms around her small, square frame.

"Who could do such a thing? It sure wasn't robbery like Trey's saying it was. Not even someone from out of town would take a look at that ramshackle place she lived in and think she had anything worth stealing." She went to the cupboard and poured herself a generous mug of Jack Daniels.

"Aggie, don't make yourself sick worrying about it. Let's wait to see what the police find out."

"She was murdered! The murderer could be right next door. They found her in her house with all those cats. They'd cut her throat—not the cats. They didn't cut her throat. Whoever killed her did that."

I shivered. "I really don't think we do ourselves any good by going over what happened. If we fixate on her murder, we'll be afraid to leave our houses." I spoke for myself. Aggie was fearless.

"Can't worry about that." Aggie zipped up the leather coat she'd worn for as long as I could remember and wound a tight gray curl around her finger. "They cut her throat!" she repeated.

"How do you know all the gory details?"

"My police scanner. I heard Trey talking to some county police officers. At first I didn't know they were talking about Elli. I nearly fainted when I figured out she was the one who was found in gallons of her own blood."

"Please, Aggie. You don't need to get so graphic. I get the picture."

"Huh?" she looked at me for only a second before she walked toward the gate. "I've got to talk to Hilda, Bub, and a few others in the old crowd. I'll let you know whatever I find out. This is just killing Hilda. She was starting to forgive Elli, you know. All that mess over a dumb bread recipe." Aggie hiked her purse back on her shoulder and scurried at race walk pace out of the yard, nearly losing her balance as she stepped into one of the many holes Messy had dug by the gate.

Elli Lundy dead—her throat slit. I slowly let the horror I'd been racing to keep ahead of sink in. In Chicago, murders happened all the time, but the big city made the most awful things seem anonymous and far away. This murder was far too close.

There was no way I was going to let myself sink into an abyss of paralytic fear. I left Messy chasing whatever phantom animal she seemed to spot as she raced around the yard. I returned to the house and my computer, intending to distract myself by searching through garbage. In other words, I was going to visit every Internet tabloid site to see what latest juicy bits had been placed to placate celebrity stalkers like me. Not one new item to take my mind away from the Cotter's Corner Killer, as my journalistically-trained mind had labeled him or her.

Dinner. Though food isn't my reason for living, it's a close second so I riffled through the Chinese and Italian menus stashed in a drawer of my newly refurbished kitchen island. Studying the long lists of high carb foods available to me, I realized I wasn't that hungry and decided to make popcorn in my air popper. I'd melt some honey and butter, lace it with Parmesan cheese, and call it a meal. It was Rose's recipe, one I'd brought back with me the last time I'd visited.

HBO seemed to be running *True Blood* on every channel, and for reasons that need not be detailed, the series, usually one of my favorites, held no appeal at the moment. I went with *The Real Housewives of New Jersey*. When you're trying to escape reality, there's nothing better than reality television.

But even those crazy women with their myriad complaints against each other didn't soothe the tingling sensations in my fingers and toes. Murder, it turns out, is a very hard thing to put out of your mind.

If you asked me, I don't think I could tell you exactly what I did for the hours before I went to bed. I suppose I flipped through the new Jane Austen biography I had just begun. And maybe I eyed my sewing machine thinking I was behind schedule for the quilt sections I'd promised Aggie. All I remember is reluctantly crawling into bed, making sure that my bedroom door was locked and that Messy was lying next to me.

I nearly ripped my bed apart tossing and turning. No amount of self talk put my anxious mind at ease. Even the antique four-poster, the one I'd had in Chicago and had once shared with Yates, whose body I inexplicably missed at that moment, didn't provide safe haven. I was full out terrified that the blackness outside my window held a person so sinister and vile that a frail eighty-year-old wasn't off limits.

I fell asleep making a mental note to remember to lock my doors when I went to work. You never know who might be crouching just outside. And, yes, there was Charley with his indelible smile.

Chapter Two

Ever since my first apartment in Chicago, bought and paid for by my stepfather Leland, my mornings have begun the same way: a small bowl of oatmeal, two cups of strong coffee, cold water thrown in my face, a brush quickly run through my sometimes too-thick-to-cooperate hair, and a short run. I'm a good runner. Though my mother's ambitions for me headed more in the tennis direction, I was an all-state, long-distance runner in my private, all-girls high school. It's my only athletic claim to fame. These days the run includes Messy, and the cold water has been topped off with some moisturizer.

As Messy and I raced, her ears flying and my hair drying, Elli's phrase *something big* pounded the pavement along with my Nikes. What did Elli know that would shake the entire town?

Back inside my house, the message light blinked on the phone as I poured kibble into my dog's bowl. As soon as I pushed "Play," Yates Logan's smooth but unwelcome voice floated from the machine.

"Hey, Sam, I have a surprise and can't think of anyone I want to share it with more than you. Please call. It's been too long." I erased the message.

He'd made partner. That was all Yates had ever wanted. I was a distant second. I knew it even when we were dating, but I stayed with him way too long. I was attractive to him because, by all accounts, I'm pretty attractive, but I also had access to the brass ring he craved: partnership in Leland's firm.

"Yates is history. I promise," I told an unconvinced-looking Messy. "He liked me because I'm the boss's stepdaughter—and maybe just a little because I'm hot," I laughed.

Messy's brown eyes stared at me in a way that told me she doubted my sanity.

I stroked her thick coat. "I'll try to get home early, but your awful grandfather probably had a very late night with a very loose lady so I'll have to do the work today." *Was it healthy to talk to a dog as much as I talked to Messy? Probably not, but she was my faithful friend, the operative word being 'faithful.'*

I poured coffee into a thermos, grabbed my car keys, but then decided the crisp November day was too beautiful to miss. I'd walk, and if the murderer chased me, I felt confident I'd be able to out run him.

Once at the office, I kept my ears and eyes open. I watched people pass and hoped I could catch a bit of what they were saying, though I knew the closed doors and windows made that impossible. People were hurrying. People never hurry in Cotter's Corner. Even stranger, today they didn't look to their left or right, just ducked into whatever store they needed to get to. Turns out I wasn't the only one terrified that the murderer might be on my doorstep.

I had bought a couple of soy lattés at Octane to Go, a little gas station and coffee shop on my way to work. One of the lattés was for Scoop, just in case he defied all odds and beat me to the office. Predictably, Scoop waltzed in an hour after I got there. I had nearly drunk both lattés.

"Hello, child of my loins." He was still in the same wrinkled clothes he'd ambled out in the afternoon before. "What's new?"

"Besides a murder? You do remember that Elli was murdered, right? Is a one-night stand all you ever think about?"

"You can't guilt me," he said. "I will never forget how Elli died. Now, how about making your pappy some real coffee?" He sneered when he looked inside my cup and saw traces of a healthy alternative to caffeine.

"That's all you have to say? I know you're the boss, but I want you to know I didn't move here from Chicago just to do your dirty work. This was supposed to be at least a fifty-fifty proposition, and I'm contributing about seventy-five percent lately."

"Nag, nag, nag. Who put the burr under your saddle?"

"Cowboy talk? You're resorting to cowboy talk? I'm no fool, Scoop. You need to lasso your share of the doggies, to use your vernacular."

"I can see why the young cowpokes aren't standing in line to poke you." He was angry and nasty.

"A low and pretty crude blow. I don't care, though, if what I said has your attention. Got it? "

"Got it." He stomped toward the backroom leaving me to wonder if I'd driven my point home or if he was merely slipping out the backdoor.

As Scoop has a tendency to do when he knows he's wrong, he returned in half an hour and said nothing about our previous conversation but began a new one. "They are having a devil of a time rounding up Elli's cats."

"I thought some friend would take them." I felt guilty that I hadn't thought much about her cats.

"Eleven cats? Who's going to take eleven cats?"

"I thought she had four or five. Eleven! How did she get eleven? No one will take eleven cats."

"There were five, but one of the cats had kittens five or six months ago. How do you think your dog would like eleven cats?" Like most of Scoop's attempts at humor, this one wasn't funny.

"I feel even worse for Elli. She lived in that decrepit house, and all she really had was those scraggly cats. Now no one wants her furry treasures. What will they do with them?"

"Over the rainbow bridge I guess. More coffee!" He waved his empty cup at me.

"They're going to kill them? You really think they'll do that?" I'm not a cat lover, but I didn't want to see them put to death as if they didn't matter, as if Elli didn't matter.

"Hey," Scoop was pouring his own coffee, "who the hell can take in a ton of cats?"

"I realize one person can't take all of them, but if we put an article in the paper—I'm sure I can find some space—maybe we'll jumpstart a movement to give Elli's cats homes."

"You're kidding, right? Advertise in my paper for tramp cats? I don't think so."

"It's *our* paper, and, besides, don't be so high and mighty. You've gone so far as to advertise used bras."

"Only to help out a friend," he grumbled under his breath.

"Now we're going to help our dearly departed friend Elli and her cats. I'll write up the ad, and then you set the type."

He beamed me a white-hot blast of fury, but he waited as I wrote the classified advertisement. Then he set the type. "I forget how much like your mother you are." It wasn't a compliment.

"Thanks," I said as if I didn't know how he meant the verbal slap in the face.

I called the animal shelter. Yes, they had the cats and, no, they wouldn't put the cats down for seven days. I promised them that I'd find the cats homes within that time. How exactly I would go about doing that was the million-dollar question. When I hung up, I realized that Scoop had managed to slip the noose and had taken off for who knew where with who knew whom.

"So, Sammie, you ready for me yet?" Charley wandered in. My face must have registered that his not-so-subtle double entendre wasn't lost on me.

In truth, his ad had totally slipped my mind, though he certainly hadn't. Elli's murder was occupying far too much of my brain space.

I went with the best defense is an offense. "Since you didn't send me the pictures and your logo, I couldn't really create the ad, could I? That may seem unreasonable to you, but to me it makes perfect sense."

"Whoa, simmer down, cute cakes. I had my assistant send them out yesterday. You didn't check your email, did you?" He leaned in, way too close.

"Well, they must have gotten lost." I got out of my chair and walked toward the coffeemaker. "Want some?" I said before I realized that my double entendre was no less subtle than his.

"I won't answer that," he smiled. "You could drive a man to distraction. What in the heck is someone like you doing in a town like this? You belong on the main stage. And by the way, how could your parents give a girl with those eyes and those lips a guy's name?"

"My mother's family name is Samuels." When I realized he hadn't taken his eyes off me, I suddenly felt very, very uncomfortable. "And Sam is the name of my father's favorite detective Sam Spade. Remember? *The Maltese Falcon*?"

"It's still a shame."

I had to break his spell or perish. "Charley, I don't know how much work you have, but I have piles of it. As much fun as this has been, I need to run to the post office and bank."

"I get the hint. Well, bye, Sammie. Since I'll be around, we'll be seeing each other, I'm sure. Send me a copy of the ad when you finish it."

For a moment, I imagined his sweet breath against my face, the feel of him enveloping me in his arms. I shook off my crazy thoughts. Shame on me. There was a murderer hovering nearby.

Then he was back.

"I mean it, you know," he said, pulling his chair up next to mine. "I'm not kidding. You're on my mind on and off pretty much all of the time since I've been back."

"Charley, if I believed that then I'd be one not so smart gal." Thank goodness my mouth still worked because my brain was frozen.

"I'm thirty three and thinking about things and people I didn't think about when I was twenty-three. There are only so many bars you can close and skirts you can chase." His look trapped me. I couldn't take my eyes off him.

"So what do you think?" He was dead serious.

"About what?" I wasn't playing coy. My mind was lost in wonderful him.

"About maybe going out sometime?"

"With you?"

"My father's a little old for you. Of course with me."

"I'm not sure that's such a good idea. I mean we have this great friendship where we share all our innermost thoughts, girlfriend."

"Don't be a smartass, Sam. I'm dead serious. Let's just go for drinks and see what happens."

"It's the 'see what happens' I'm worried about," I said, thinking that those were probably the same words my father used to lure my young, unsuspecting mother toward years of misery.

"No guts no glory, sweetie. How about it?"

"I guess."

"I'll take that for a *yes*."

"I have to ask. Why are you all of a sudden so interested?"

"I told you. It's not all of a sudden, and maybe I'm finally growing up."

"It's still hard to believe. You've always managed to have any woman you want, and you've become the talk of the town doing it. Suddenly, here you are inviting me for drinks."

"Maybe it's the elusive butterfly of love, baby." His hand rested on my shoulder. "And you were dating that sharpshooter from Chicago, remember? I'm a lot of things, but I'm not a guy who steps in on another guy's territory."

"Unless he's married to the woman, right?" I knew immediately I'd overstepped my bounds.

"Don't believe everything you hear, ok? I'm a pretty good boy." His smile was gone.

I let out a breath, realizing it had been too long since I'd taken one. "Ok."

"So when do you want to go for that drink?"

"I have a pretty busy week or two," I lied. "Keep your nose clean, and we'll see what we can come up with."

"Keep my nose clean, huh? Sure, Mom, that's what I'll do. And after the drink, I'll show you my place."

"Uh, not on the first date," I squirmed.

"Not my house, my business. We're getting the showroom ready."

"You do take this seriously, don't you?" It was one of those comments that darted out of my mouth with absolutely no stop at my brain.

"My dad taught his boy to take work and women both very seriously."

"Right." I wanted to believe him, but there was very little supporting evidence.

"Before you go," I searched through the files on my desk to find the makeshift one I'd put together for Charley's ad, "is there anything else you can think of you want in your ad?"

"Dazzle me," he called over his shoulder as he walked toward the door.

"I'll put it on the Internet too. We've just started an online edition." The door closed before I finished the sentence. "Dazzle me," he'd said. Dazzle me, he had.

Now I'd done it. It might be the murderer or the stars in misalignment because the one thing I vowed never to do, I'd just done. I'd given Charley the idea that we would go out. For years, I'd promised myself two things: I'd never bungee jump, and I'd never open the door to a relationship with Charley Cotter. And the former was still safer than the latter. What was I thinking, and what was I thinking with?!

At that moment Scoop resurfaced. "Saw the Cotter snot walking out of here."

"He wants us to run an ad. For a man who's so secretive about his own love life, you're certainly nosy about mine."

"You'd better be kidding about Charley Cotter having anything to do with your love life."

"Chill. He was really just here for business."

"Well, no monkey business. I don't want my daughter to be another notch on his cummerbund."

"Not your business." It wasn't, but there was something inexplicably reassuring about his actually seeming to care who I dated. He wasn't wild about Yates, I knew that, but Charley evoked even more violent feelings in Scoop. Ever since that summer, Scoop hated Charley and made sure that wherever I went after that, Charley was nowhere near.

"Charles Cotter, Senior, is one of the richest men in the country and he spoiled his only kid to death. I don't like Junior Cotter. Never have. Never will. He can't be trusted."

"That's probably how mother's family felt about you." I couldn't help myself. He'd made it too easy.

"Out of bounds," he snapped. "But they were right to feel that way, and I am, too."

It was perhaps the first time my father had admitted any wrongdoing where my mother was concerned.

"All Charley wants to do is go for drinks."

"You're kidding, right?"

"Right." Why fight a battle before it's necessary? Besides the very smooth Charley Cotter might not have been serious. The thought made me realize how much I hoped he was.

"There are lots of fish in the sea. And you're a catch." He threw off the last sentence, but it rocked me. It wasn't like him to say nice things to or about me. I hoped he hadn't just been diagnosed with a terminal illness.

*****

Predictably, Scoop was there less than an hour. I was again left with copyediting and ads to create. This was getting real old real fast. I emailed my mother. Next, I left a phone message for Yates because guilt had gotten to me and I did owe him a return call. All I said was that I was happy for his promotion, but that we had nothing left to say to each other. Then I walked down the block to Mabel's Restaurant hoping Lacy was there to fill me in on all the latest gossip.

Lacy Pickett is my closest friend in town since I started spending my summers with Scoop the summer after second grade. "He doesn't care about her, he just wants to lessen his financial burden," I heard my mother telling a friend when my father won custody for two-and-a-half months every summer. For the longest time, I believed her.

"I was just about to call you." Lacy was there with her beautiful face and welcoming smile. "God, Sam, I feel just awful about Elli. I tell you it creeps me out when I think that there I am in my little house at the end of nowhere all by myself."

"All by yourself?" I knew that any number of men kept my Halle Berry-lookalike friend company.

"Okay, not always by myself—but enough that I'm really jittery. Trey was here a while ago, and what he said gave me the heebie-jeebies." I hated that Lacy actually seemed head over heels about arrogant, worthless Trey. I hoped he was merely her man of the moment and that her infatuation with our local constabulary would pass as quickly as any number of her flings. "He said they have no clue who did it or why. It's scary as hell, isn't it? Yikes, I'd better change the subject, or I'll have to go home and hide under the covers. You want the usual, I suppose?" I nodded, and she left to prepare my order: an avocado, sprout, Havarti, and tomato sandwich on homemade oatmeal bread with cucumber dressing. I always top it off with my standard drink: Mabel's authentic-soda-fountain green river soda.

"Scoop is betting it's robbery," I said as I stood at the counter watching Lacy assemble my sandwich.

"Wouldn't I love to be the one to tell that creaky Casanova that he's dead wrong. No robbery. Nothing was taken, not even the five one-hundred dollar bills that Elli had on her chest of drawers. Trey told me."

"He's going around telling everyone else to keep quiet, and he's shooting off his mouth."

"Now, now," she said. "I know you don't like him, but on this you have to give him a break. He's frantically trying to stop someone else from being murdered."

"It's still so hard to believe that something that awful could happen here."

"Beyond awful." For a second, Lacy stopped slathering cucumber dressing onto the oatmeal bread. "Hey, give me a second, and I'll join you." She quickly finished assembling the sandwich and handed it to me along with my drink.

"Nutritious," I said studying her lunch as she sat across from me: a chocolate cupcake and mocha latté. The girl had no reason to be so outrageously fit.

"Most all of the major food groups," she laughed.

"I'm not wild about the thought of a murderer in our neighborhood," I confessed as I bit into the perfect sandwich. "I admit, I've started scrutinizing everyone—except you, of course."

"Of course," she laughed. "Oops. Aunt Mabel just came in. Gotta go or she'll fire me faster than she fires up that greasy grill. Stay safe."

Lacy leapt from her chair, leaving half a cupcake and most of her latté.

"You stay safe too." Once again I felt grateful that Lacy had befriended me all those summers ago. Years later, she told me she sought me out because she knew what it was to be lonely. To most of the people in Cotter's Corner, she was known as the girl whose father was in prison for killing her mother in a fit of jealous rage.

Back at the paper, I balanced the accounts from the previous week. I then went to my email hoping that Charley was wrong, that he hadn't sent me the information I needed. But there it was, right in my inbox.

Just why had Charley been the man of my dreams and nightmares for way too long? His charm and looks, though ample, weren't unique. In Chicago, good looking, charismatic men are a dime a dozen. Yates, in fact, was a showstopper, the kind of man women turned to look at. It was that darn night at the lake at a time in a girl's life that created moments to remember.

I totally got that Scoop hates Charley because Charley is a younger, much less grumpy version of himself. He sees in Charley his own inconstancy and unreliability where women are concerned. But Charley, Jr., is not like Scoop. There are no surreptitious addictions and no three marriages by the time he was only a few years older than Charley.

The next few days kept me occupied with work and finding homes for Elli's cats. Aggie, Hilda, and Bub had all taken one, as had several members of Elli's church. The ad I placed with the darling clipart kitty had enticed several more cat lovers to add to their furry families. Only three remained, and I hoped they'd all find loving homes so I didn't have to take a cat. Messy would never forgive me.

Most of my nights were spent mentally wandering to all things distracting and threatening. In my dark bedroom, I thought about the murderer. I couldn't help it. No one had been identified as the perpetrator, and everyone seemed on edge. I couldn't help wondering if what happened to Elli was only the tip of the iceberg. All too soon I would have the horrifying answer.

Chapter Three

Good old Aggie! When I got home from work a few days later, there on my doorstep were half a dozen issues of *The National Enquirer.* I quickly shoved them inside my jacket so that the neighbors, if any were around, wouldn't see my true reading pleasures. *I adore those sinful treasures,* I told myself—anything to get my mind off Elli's murder.

"Messy girl, we're going to have a great night with junk food and gossip." My life as Leland Henry's stepdaughter showered me with drawers full of expensive jewelry, closets full of designer clothes, trips all over the world, and a trust fund that ensures that I work only because I feel I should. But it's trash reading I love.

As soon as I fed and watered Messy, I plopped down on my ultra-soft, ultra-comfortable leather sectional to read the magazines and shove peanut M&Ms into my mouth. Just as I was beginning to feel a tinge guilty for again delaying sewing Aggie's quilt squares, the phone rang. In a moment of reckless abandon, I answered it. Big mistake.

"Sam, dear, it's your mother."

"Mom, I know your voice." Being Mrs. Leland Henry has negatively impacted the woman who once made all my clothes and baked the bread for my peanut butter sandwiches. Now she's Mrs. Somebody from her well-tended toes to her perfectly-sculpted platinum blonde hair. I liked MBL (Mother Before Leland) better than this expensive but superficial model.

"Are you in a bad mood? You sound peevish?"

Peevish? Who says "peevish"? "No, I just got home and haven't settled in yet." Lie. Lie. Lie.

"I just wanted to see if Yates has given you his good news. Leland and I are so proud of him."

"We haven't talked. I left him a message saying that I already knew he'd been made partner and congratulated him. It's easier than talking to him. No matter how much I tell him I don't want to have any contact, he doesn't get it."

"Samuels," she never uses my formal name unless she's close to shouting, "you are so fortunate that, after all you've put him through, he still wants to connect to you."

"Put *him* through? All I did was decide not to marry his boring self. I'm not sure that constitutes putting him through anything." Now I was close to shouting. "Yates is old news. Like you and Scoop." To my mother, bringing up my father's name was akin to shouting.

"Ridiculous!" Shouting. "Unlike the aforementioned dirt bag, Yates Logan is a faithful, brilliant, hardworking, and very handsome attorney whom many young women might consider the greatest catch in Chicago."

"Take a breath, Mother."

"I hate it when we argue," she sounded on the verge of tears, "but I would have killed to have found someone like Yates. Oh, I love Leland, you know I do, but we have had our little trials."

Yes, I did know about those trials that usually come in the form of shapely twenty-somethings that my mother gets wind of from one of her faux friends. "I give you credit for perseverance, Mother. No matter how many times I tell you that Yates Logan will never be more to me than a distant memory, you still hammer away that he and I belong together."

"He'll always be honorable. That's all I'm saying." She said it in her most theatrical voice.

"Messy is faithful. I'll stick with her." *And I won't have to be bought off by a big thick diamond bracelet or dripping-with-diamonds earrings several times a year*, I thought to myself.

"All I meant to say, sweetie, is that I have learned misplaced pride doesn't put nice cars in the garage or fat checks in personal savings accounts. Remember, I was poor and proud once. We both were. It wasn't fun, was it?"

"But thanks to you and Leland, I'm not, and probably won't ever be short of money. Yates can't offer me anything I can't get myself." I hated talking about money—the money that was stashed in bank accounts piling interest upon interest because I hardly ever touched it.

"He would make a devoted husband and father." She was as fierce and determined as Messy was when I gave her a rawhide bone.

"Devoted but absent. His children and wife will never see his workaholic self," I said wishing we weren't playing in virtual marriage land. My mother goes there frequently.

My mother yammered on, piling up guilt like the interest on my money. She had once had a hard life, and I knew she made many of her decisions because she was determined to give me a better one. Her mother had died when she was born, and her father handed her off to her Aunt Cathy, a Mennonite living with her inflexible, religious-zealot of a husband. It couldn't have been easy for my petite, beautiful mother to be shackled to a life of hard work and no fun. No wonder she made a break for it when the first opportunity presented itself. Too bad it came in the form of my father.

"Mother, I know you want what's best for me. I just think that at thirty, I probably should decide that for myself."

"You can be so unforgiving and cold at times." She sniffled into the phone. She was pulling out the big guns to get me to relent on my Yates' doctrine.

"Remember Charley Cotter?" Bringing up Charley was only partly to change the subject. It was also to get back a little at my mother for her intrusions into my life.

"What does Charley Cotter have to do with our conversation? You're not dating him are you?" Ice.

"Charley? No, I'm not dating him."

"You've never dated him, have you?"

"No," I said as if it were the farthest thing from my mind.

"I only brought him up because I talked to him a day or so ago," I added, "and you'll be happy to hear that he's becoming more responsible. You really don't know him as well as you think you do." *And you certainly don't know he saved my life when he hauled me from that rip current.*

"Hear me when I say this, and hear me loud and clear," my mother's voice ballooned to drill-instructor proportions. "I know enough to know that I never want to know Charley Cotter any better than I do this minute. He took advantage of a sixteen-year-old girl. He is trash. Rich trash, but trash."

"Oh, I think I forgot to tell you, there was a murder here a week or so ago?" I said it to scare and shock her because she'd been unfair to Charlie, though why I felt the need to defend him I didn't know.

"Murder? In Cotter's Corner?" The unadulterated fear in her voice told me I'd gone too far in order to get back at her for the Charley attack.

"It's not as bad as it sounds. The woman was elderly, and it might not be a murder." I didn't think I'd go to hell for not telling my mother the complete truth about Elli if it was to keep her from sleepless nights.

"I worry about you," she sounded sad. "You're drifting away. I see you starting to make the same kinds of mistakes that I made."

"I'm fine, and I'll be fine. You know I'm still the smart, sturdy girl you raised. No mistakes made here."

"Promise you'll keep using that good head on your shoulders?"

"Promise. I'll call in a couple of days. Love you, and tell Leland I said 'hello'." There was no way I could tell her to give Leland my love because I just didn't love him. I'd tried. I really had.

My life, I thought after I hung up, is full of highly complicated relationships: my mother, my father, Charley—if you could call what we had a relationship—and Leland.

For me, summers in Cotter's Corner became the one constant in my life, and Scoop, irregular as he was, showed in unspoken ways that he did love me. So when the Princeton acceptance came and I chose DePaul in order to have at least a little time around familiar things, Scoop stood up for me against my mother and Leland's protestations that the Ivy League was where I belonged—the golden key to a golden future. That was the first time I considered that Scoop wanted me close, and Chicago was a whole lot closer than New Jersey was.

But my mother still hated Charley. That was never more obvious than the phone conversation I'd just ended. Yeah, I was wise not to tell her that drinks with Charley were a definite possibility, made more possible by her prejudice against him. My mother wasn't that good a judge of men; still, I worried I wasn't either.

To get my mind off the stressful phone call, I dashed off an email to Rose promising her I'd seriously consider a Christmas visit. As an afterthought, I cut and pasted an article on Elli's murder. Rose had a cast iron stomach, and since we'd bonded over sensationalism and our love for Stephen King and Janet Evanovich, I knew Rose's recent baby blues would totally dissolve at my detailing the murderous goings-on in Cotter's Corner. I'd probably find her on my doorstep, oozing questions about the grisly crime.

My duties were done. I let Messy in and went into the den and my sewing stash. I pulled out the box of various shapes and sizes of quilting pieces. Went to the kitchen where Aunt Cathy's old Singer sat in its cabinet at one corner. "This helps so much," Aggie says every time I hand her a quilt top. "Rheumatism has made it harder and harder for me to keep up and the church needs these."

I had sewn four, nine-inch squares of the Yellow Brick Road pattern Aggie's church ladies had decided on when the phone rang. "Sam, come quick," Lacy cried into the phone. "I need you. Aunt Mabel is dead!" Then the phone, too, went dead.

As I drove like a bat out of hell to get to Lacy's aunt's restaurant, I remembered that I hadn't asked Lacy how Mabel Pollock died. It didn't matter. I already knew.

Chapter Four

No matter what horrifying images I'd conjured up on my way to help Lacy, the reality was far more sickening and terrible. Police cars lined the street. Because one of the auxiliary police officers recognized me, I was allowed to go in.

Lacy sat slumped and weeping at a corner table in the far left of the room. In the right corner, behind the blood-spattered counter and wall, the police huddled around Mabel Pollock's lifeless body. I turned away in order to avoid seeing any more.

"Get over there with Lacy!" Trey Davis shouted at me. I went to my friend.

"It's so awful. How could this have happened? It's my fault." Her words fell on top of each other. "I'm going crazy, aren't I, Sam? I mean no one would do this to my aunt!"

Truthfully, as I hugged her and let her sob convulsively into my polar fleece jacket, I could think of any number of people who'd probably imagined doing away with the hard-bitten, demanding Mabel. There wasn't a server she hadn't reduced to tears or one of her renters that she hadn't threatened to kick to the curb the minute the rent was late.

And she certainly had never been my favorite. More than once, Lacy's aunt had screamed at her to hang up when she and I were in the middle of a conversation. Once she shouted me off her porch saying, "Rich lazy white girl from Chicago, ain't you got nothing better to do than keep my Lacy from getting to work." Mabel's explosive temper was legendary. Stories circulated through town about her firing people at will. She'd also been known to evict tenants from one of her many apartment houses just because she felt like it or because she get could get more money from another paying customer. Finding who wanted to murder Mabel might be easier than finding someone who didn't.

"Aunt Mabel let me off early to do my laundry and meet someone for drinks," Lacy lowered her voice and looked in the direction of Trey, which told me he was not the person she'd been meeting. "I decided to check on her before going out for the evening. That's where I found her." Lacy's entire body shook as she pointed toward her aunt's body.

"It's going to be all right. It is." It was if I were standing outside myself watching everything but not connecting. "Let's get you out of here." I gathered up Lacy's bag and keys.

"I don't know," again she looked in Trey's direction. "I'm not sure I can leave yet."

I felt like I was taking my life in my hands by walking up to Trey, but I needed to get Lacy away from the stomach-churning scene.

"Didn't I tell you to stay over there?" His severe facial features looked even more angular and unappealing.

I didn't give him time to finish his angry rant. "I need to know if it's okay to take Lacy to my house."

"Go ahead. I'll talk to her some more tomorrow." Trey was always an overbearing creep, but tonight I'd cut him some slack.

I hurried Lacy to my car, and though she insisted she could be by herself, I ignored her. She wasn't hungry and within minutes of our getting to my house, she was asleep on my sofa. I placed one of Aggie's handmade quilts over her and closed the door to the family room so she could rest.

I, on the other hand, could not. Messy lay snoring next to me, but after three cups of coffee, I was wide awake with every grim detail of the night soaking in. I went back downstairs and dialed.

"Mabel's dead," I whispered into the phone.

"What?" Scoop must have been sleeping, I put out of my mind whether or not there was someone with him. "Sam, did you say Mabel's dead?"

"I have Lacy here. The police are still at the restaurant. It was awful."

"Lock your doors. I'll go down to the restaurant. My god, what's going on?"

I don't know if I slept more than an hour or so, but I woke early, wanting to be the first one up so Lacy wouldn't become confused and panicked when she found herself in a strange house and remembered what had happened the night before.

But Lacy was already up and sitting at the table staring vacantly out the window when I walked in the kitchen. Messy lay on the floor next to her.

"How are you doing?" I asked as hugged her. "This will get better you know."

"Everything is so unreal," she said. "Right now it's hard to believe anything will ever be all right again."

"I called Aggie. She'll feed Scylla," I said. "She's going to stop here for a key. I wasn't worried about letting him out because I remembered that you have a doggy door."

"Aunt Mabel's really dead, isn't she?"

"She is, Lace. I'm so sorry. I don't know what to do to help you. Let me fix us something to eat. I'm sure I have eggs and cheese. I'll whip up an omelet, one of the benefits of the kids' cooking camp my mother sent me to."

"Thanks. But I'm not hungry. Do what you have to do today. Don't worry about me. I already talked to

Trey and told him everything I know. I called the funeral home, and they will see that Aunt Mabel is cremated. There won't be a service. They said she'd made arrangements. I guess she did that a few months ago. Odd that she didn't tell me."

"I'll do anything you need me to. You know that."

"Thanks. I have so much guilt, Sam. I wasn't all that good to her, and now look what's happened." She pressed her hands against her eyes, as if that would somehow stop the tears flowing torrentially down her cheeks.

"You were terrific to her," I insisted, "and she loved you more than she loved anyone. We all knew that. Don't start beating yourself up. You didn't kill her. Be mad at the person who did."

"Do you think it was the same person who killed Elli? What would Elli and my aunt have in common that the same person would want to murder them? Murder! It sounds so awful to say someone you loved was murdered."

I know Lacy was thinking about what her father did to her mother, but I let it alone. "Look who I found starting to ring your doorbell." Aggie walked in with Charley.

"Sorry to barge in but I needed to see that you're all right." He sat down next to his old friend Lacy who immediately fell against him. "That's what I thought. You're pretty wiped out, aren't you, sweetie?" Charley was perfect with her, gentle and loving and patient. If I weren't half in love with him already, this show of tenderness would have done the trick.

"The scanner told me what happened," Aggie spoke rapid fire. "I don't know what this town's coming to. We're dropping like flies, and no one seems to be able to find out who's slaughtering us."

"Aggie," I had to get her off her gory monologue, "how about you make your wonderful pancakes for us? I'll help. Lacy says she's not hungry, but I bet we can change her mind."

For the next few minutes, Charley talked to Lacy about what she needed to do next, and I helped Aggie find the ingredients for her pancakes. Lucky for all of us that Aggie was making the pancakes. I didn't exactly tell the whole truth about the kids' cooking camp. Turns out there were a few kids who lacked the culinary artistry gene, and I was one of them. My pancakes were inedible. Not even the instructor had the courage to try them. Thankful for Aggie's intervention, I put the griddle on the stove, handed the pancake turner to her, and poured more coffee for everyone.

"Much as I would love to stay," Charley rose from his chair, "I need to get to work."

"You work?" Aggie spoke in an icy tone. "How nice."

He ignored Aggie's sarcasm, gave Lacy a kiss on the cheek, and turned to me, "I'll call you later today and see what you need," he said. I walked with him to his car parked in the driveway. Messy was in her yard probably glad to be away from everyone.

"You'll think this is odd because I do," he said as began to unlock his car, "but when I heard what happened to Mabel, I had an almost irrational urge to see how you were. I drove over here a few hours ago, but all the lights were out. It took great restraint, but I waited until it looked like someone was up."

"That's sweet. You're a very nice person, Charley, no matter what anyone says."

"Very funny. Always the kidder," he stepped toward me. "Can we be just a little serious for a few moments?"

I nodded.

"I have always had an interest in you, and I think you've had times that you could have been interested in me, if I hadn't been too wild or too caught up in being stupid. This may be the right time for both of us to get on the same page and see if there's anything we might cobble together to make a relationship."

He was saying exactly what he'd said in every dream I'd ever had about him, but the reality of his words terrified me. "Charley, you've met my mother a couple of times. If I told her I was thinking of taking you more seriously, it might kill her. And if I told Scoop I was going out with you, he might kill me."

"So you aren't interested?" he stopped for a minute. "Be careful what you say because it might be the beginning of something wonderful or the death of something that never got a chance to be wonderful."

"Could you not use the word death?" I laughed nervously.

"You promised we'd be serious for a minute."

"Oh, Charley, you know I wish it could be different. I *have* wondered what it would be like to date you, but I'm nearly thirty. I'm not that love-starved little girl anymore."

"And that's exactly why I'm asking you to consider going out with me."

And before I knew what happened, he kissed me briefly but definitely on the lips. "Call me when you figure out your answer. Oh, and tell your mother hello from me when you talk to her."

His kiss left me weak, my legs wobbled as I went back to the house. What I'd do next was anybody's guess.

Lacy smiled when I returned. "I'm telling Aggie that these are the absolute best pancakes I've ever had."

"Lemon lime soda," Aggie said proudly. "It makes them light and fluffy. It's an old family recipe. Here, Snoopy, sit down and I'll get you some."

I sat next to Lacy who was devouring the pancakes. "I'm going to have to get your recipe and put them on the menu. I'll call them "Aggie's Pancakes.""

Aggie beamed as she boldly flipped a pancake.

"Are there calls you need me to make, Lacy? I'm good at organizing and running errands. Let me." I needed to be busy, to take my mind off that kiss.

"No one really. It was only Aunt Mabel and me. The rest of the family is pretty scattered and dysfunctional. "Is it okay if I take a bath and borrow some clothes?" she asked. "And I'm hoping you have an extra toothbrush." She again looked confused and heartbroken. "Sorry I'm such a mess," she half laughed and half cried.

"Here's an extra toothbrush," I saw when we were upstairs in the guest bedroom. "I'll go grab some jeans and tops for you to look over and see what you want to wear."

"Thanks," she said as I handed her towels and the toothbrush. "What makes you think I'm doing well?" she asked.

"Because you ate all your pancakes." I smiled. "And mine, too."

"What am I going to do without her?" Lacy brushed her hair from her face and wiped away tears. "I'm sorry I can't get it together, but I feel so alone."

"You know we love you, right?" I said. "You're the most loved girl in town."

"I wonder what would have happened if I'd gotten there earlier. Would the murderer have killed me too? Or maybe I could have saved her?"

"Those thoughts don't do you any good. What happened *happened*." I sounded far more in charge than I felt.

"She was just lying there. It didn't even look like her." Lacy shook her head as if trying to shake the thoughts away.

"Lacy . . . " I wanted to keep her from reliving the horror she'd experienced the night before but couldn't find the words.

"All that blood," she buried her face in her hands. "Trey told me that it was a robbery, but I know it was more than that."

"He thinks Elli was robbed too," I said. "But what makes you sure Mabel wasn't murdered during a robbery?"

"She'd been upset about something for days. I asked her what was wrong, but she refused to tell me."

"Do you think she had any financial trouble, anyone she owed money?"

"Aunt Mabel with money trouble? No way. That restaurant is a little goldmine. Besides, she was loaded. I guess when Uncle Leroy was killed in the granary explosion, there was a huge settlement. Aunt Mabel told me she never touched it, just left it in the bank to gather interest. Can you imagine? He's been gone nearly thirty years. That's a lot of interest. No, she didn't have any money problems. Something else was bothering her. I heard her on the phone a couple of days ago. She was yelling her head off. She had a temper, a bad one, but this was different. I'd never heard her scream that loudly. When I asked her who it was, she told me that I didn't need to know. What she really said was that it was none of my business. Well, one good thing may come out of all this bad. Charley is sure paying attention to you. It's about time!"

"He's being a good friend." I shrugged off her words. "And it's you he's worried about."

"This is Lacy you're talking to." She put her hands on my shoulders. "I've watched the two of you stumbling around for years, drooling over each other. That dull ex of yours is history, and it seems that Charley has stopped dipping his toe and other parts of himself in married waters. He's decided to grab the brass ring. Let him, Sam. Drop your guard, and be the girl I know you are. There's no way that you'll become your mother, and there's no way that darling, loving man who walked out of here is your flawed father."

"Let's get your life straightened out before we fix mine, okay?"

"Promise me you won't be—you! Lose that fear that something awful happens if you let go."

I wasn't sure Lacy was the one to guide my love life, but I hoped what she was saying was right. More and more, I thought it might be the time for Charley and me. I would call and tell him I wanted to go on a real date. I would. Thanks to what had happened in town lately, I was learning that life is too short to have regrets of things left undone.

I showered, threw on some sweats and met Lacy in the kitchen.

"I called the community college in Grand Rapids. Aunt Mabel didn't want a service so I'm going to use the money to endow a scholarship for women interested in starting their own business. If you don't mind, I'm going to stay here today and watch old movies."

"Then that's what we'll do." I said.

"No, you're going to work. I'm fine here by myself," Lacy insisted.

"Hey, what do you mean you're staying here by yourself? I like old movies too, don't I, Sammie?" Aggie put an arm around Lacy.

I nodded to assure Lacy that what Aggie told her was true. "But I want to help too," I said.

"You have," Lacy took my hand. "I think I'm done crying for a while. And Trey's coming by after work."

Trey's coming to my house didn't make my heart sing, but if that would make Lacy feel better, I'd grin and bear it.

Truthfully, I could use the time to finish the monthly billing, and I needed to put a couple more items in *Snooping*. Maybe people downtown would be gossiping about the murder. I was hungry for more information.

"And think about what I said." Lacy gave me a wink.

"About?" Aggie asked.

"Oh," Lacy said, "I told her that Charley is worth considering."

"You're going through a lot," Aggie was gentle but firm, "so I'll chalk your bad advice up to that. Our Sam and Charley don't belong in the same world. He changes women like I change underpants." Her eyes shot me a look that could freeze molten lava.

"We were just talking," I said. "I need to get going."

"Just remember," Aggie wasn't finished. "He helps himself to anything and anyone he wants. He's back, but only for a while. Soon he'll take off for another tropical spot full of skimpy bikinis and skimpier morals. Ask your mother how much fun it is to be married to a man who's married to his own ego."

Leave it to Aggie to pop the romance balloon. And a huge part of me knew she was right. Charley was bad news in pretty much every way, but Lacy knows him and she knows me, and she doesn't think our getting together is a bad idea. Maybe Aggie was right—Lacy wasn't thinking straight because of what she'd just gone through. I hoped it was more than that, though. I wanted to believe that Lacy knew exactly what she was doing and saying.

Chapter Five

The cats all had homes. It was good news for me and even better for Messy who would have required treatment for clinical depression if a feline had been allowed to encroach on her territory. Great! One worry out of the way. Now I could tackle a hundred others.

"The plot sure has thickened, hasn't it?" Scoop's eyes were as red as his fire engine red flannel shirt.

"What have you found out?" I watched him struggle to steady his hands in order to pour another cup of coffee.

"Shock of shocks, Trey has no clue as to who offed Mabel. Imagine that. He did say that it was the most violent crime scene he'd ever worked."

"I'm betting Mabel's murder is only the second crime scene he ever worked, unless you count the bed bug epidemic at the no-tell motel."

"I forgot he used to be a pest inspector." Scoop spilled coffee on himself.

"Lacy was in a little better shape when I left her. Charley Cotter stopped in for a while, and Aggie is going to stay with her until I get home."

"Poor kid. Nothing has ever come easy for her. And Mabel sure wasn't a tender, lovin' caregiver, but without her, Lacy's life would have been a total mess. Why's Cotter hanging around?"

"He was there for Lacy. They go way back. Now that you're rooting around in my private life, do I get to nose around in yours? If I do, how about telling me why you look like death warmed over."

"No sleep," he smirked. "Bet you thought you caught me coming off a bender, but no such luck, dutiful daughter. I was up most of the night contacting my sources in the FBI and state police. Trey was barely able to handle one murder. Now that we have two, help has to be on its way. I called old pals to see what they know, and when they can get involved. The answer is that they've offered help, but so far Trey and the county sheriff say they've got it covered."

"You're kidding?"

"Nope. Trey isn't competent enough to recognize his own incompetence. I'll keep after them though. I don't want a third murder; nobody does, especially if it's one of us, right?"

"Right." *Right.*

"And just to guilt you and make you feel ashamed of doubting your dear old dad, I joined AA a couple of weeks ago. If you'd cared to notice, you would have seen that I'm not drinking. Just tired."

"So that's why you're at that coffee pot all the time."

"I figure a caffeine addiction is safer. Now let me get back to work. Someone has to make sure this business doesn't go down the toilet."

Scoop was trying to stop drinking. I hoped there wasn't something wrong, that the doctor hadn't told him he had only days to live, because I could think of no other reason that the man whose aftershave was Bud Lite would give up one of his two favorite preoccupations.

"Proud of you," I said as an afterthought, without looking up from the papers on my desk.

"Change of subject," he seemed to be speaking from under a pile of papers. "I've got a wild idea that might work. You're really good with that computer and know a lot about social networking. What if we do something like they do in those old detective shows? What if we plant evidence or something to draw out the criminal? We could put something in the online blog you've been working on. Lots of people read those things, maybe one of them will be the person who killed Elli and Mabel."

"Truthfully? I think you're living your Sam Spade alter ego. And it scares me to think of it," I said. "But if I did put it on the blog, I could also mention it on Facebook. If someone around here is committing the murders, it could cause him to show himself."

He nodded. "Well, think about it. I'll keep working on the idea, too. It might not be such a good thing because we could end up drawing out a bunch of kooks, but it's about all we can do. Now if you don't mind, I'll get to work so I can go home and catch a few hours sleep."

Scoop left midday, but phone calls and drop-ins kept me an hour longer than I wanted to be there. Aggie called to tell me that she and Lacy had ordered pizza and were watching DVDs. She said Trey had called and said he couldn't stop by, that Mabel's murder was loading him down with paperwork. Trust Trey to make a murder more about the burden on him than the burden on Lacy.

Left to myself, I had the time to do something I'd had on my mind: stop by Elli's. I figured that Trey's focus would be on Mabel's murder for a few days, giving me time to go to Elli's and see if I could find something that might have been overlooked.

Elli's small shambles of a house is at the edge of town, at the north end of Newton's Forest, a state forest owned by Michigan Tech. Elli sold her couple of acres and the house to the university half a dozen years ago, and they let her live there rent free. She certainly wasn't killed for her money. All she had besides a very small pension was the money she made from her bread sales and from the Bingo games which she seemed to win an unbelievable number of times, always when she was down to her last dollar. Her customers surreptitiously overpaid for the bread, and someone always finagled the Bingo game for Elli to win at least once a night. Cotter's Corner, a couple of murders excepted, is a very nice town full of very kind people.

I was right. The crime scene was far from clean. In fact, the door had been left unlocked. Once inside, it took me a minute or so to get used to the eye-stinging smell of cat urine and the unmistakable smell of Elli— part Ivory Soap, part Ban deodorant. It was lonely there without her.

As I walked through the small, dusty rooms filled with ragged furniture and cheap knickknacks, I felt sad. I also felt an almost crippling fear that her murderer lurked very close by. Elli had been murdered in the living room where I was now standing. Someone had probably sneaked up on her and killed her before she realized what was happening. At least, that was the way I hoped it happened. I couldn't bear to think of how terrified Elli would be if she'd spotted her killer.

My eyes darted from corner to corner, searching for a figure crouched and ready to strike. Once I assured myself that I was safe, I resumed my walkthrough. Though the house was once littered with worthless trinkets, many bare spots indicated that objects had already been removed. Her total loser nephew Burt wasn't above ransacking the place for anything worth a buck before Elli's body was cold. No one in town had any respect for him. Most avoided Burt Lundy like the plague.

No obvious clues jumped out at me, no suspicious notes were left half written. Miss Marple was SOL.

Suddenly a noise scared the bejesus out of me. I flinched. The harder I listened, though, the more I recognized that the noise wasn't from a sinister force, but more likely a frightened animal. Oh no, one of Elli's cats had been left behind. And there she was.

Huddled in a corner was Elli's beloved Legs. A year or so ago, she'd found a kitten in an alley. When Elli took it to her vet, the vet had urged her to put the kitten down. "It's leg is too badly injured," the veterinarian gently told her. "I'll have to amputate. No one wants a three-legged cat." But the vet was wrong. Elli took the little cat into her house and heart. Without Elli's knowing, I'd arranged with the vet to pay the bill, asking him to tell Elli that it was from a fund set up for neglected animals. Then I'd started a fund for neglected animals that the vet would administer for future needs.

"I named her Legs," Elli had told Aggie and me. "It's not for the obvious reason of her having only three legs. I named her after the gangster Legs Diamond. He was a rough guy. I thought it would build her confidence to have a name like that."

Elli was a tough bird on the outside but a total marshmallow inside. "Poor little thing. What are you doing here?" I bent to pet Legs who immediately began purring loudly and desperately. "Have you been hiding from everyone? I wish you could talk. I bet you could find Elli's killer, couldn't you?" *That shiftless Burt. He probably knew she was here and didn't even care.*

"You look like you're starving." I held her to me. "I think we need to get you to Dr. Sherrod. She'll make sure you're okay. Then I'll take you to Friends of Animals so that they can find you a nice home." No way would I take her to Burt. He'd have a much crueler solution as to what to do with Legs. She was a sweet cat. I'd get her checked out and then see if Lacy wanted a kitty. Probably not. Her French bulldog Scylla was rumored far and wide to hate cats, having treed several and scared others half to death.

"So . . . " the voice stopped my heart. It was loud and immediately recognizable. There was a reason that Scoop called Burt Lundy, "Burp" Lundy. Burt stood there in all his fat, sloppy, unkempt glory. "What brings you here?" he asked, looking at the part of me that doesn't include my face, if you get my drift.

Both Burt Lundy's work shirt and pants were borderline filthy. Above the left pocket of his shirt was stamped "Moe's Garage." No one in town was dumb enough to hire Burt to fix a car, but Moe Dahlgren was a member of Elli's church with a big heart so he found small jobs for Elli's ex-felon nephew. As far as Elli was concerned, Burt was her nephew in name only. His daughter Jenny was the love and light of Elli's life. Like most of the town, I kept my distance from the sinister creep.

"I was just walking by." I started to give him a lengthier explanation but decided against it. "I found Legs."

"Yeah. That's why I'm here. Gonna take the cat to the pound. When I tried to catch it earlier, damn thing ran from me. I brought these gloves and this bag. Don't want to get scratched and get infected."

You or the cat? Hard to believe Burt wasn't infected by just about everything already. His skin was sallow and his pupils were totally dilated.

"Oh, no!" I shouted as he began to take the cat from me and place it in the bag. I knew he was going to drown it in the lake. No way would he take the time to get Legs to the shelter.

"Just gonna use this sack to get it to the pound," he looked down as he spoke, a sure sign of lying. "I'm allergic or I'd take him." *Liar. Liar.* "Jenny's allergic, too, so I can't have a cat there when she visits." *Pants on fire.* Everyone knew his beautiful daughter had steered clear of him for years for reasons I didn't have the stomach to contemplate. After Burt's long suffering wife died, ten-year-old Jenny had been semi-adopted by her mother's preacher and his wife. Elli had told Aggie she'd considered adopting Jenny, but didn't have the strength to fight Burt for custody. And Elli admitted that at that time, she was still partying too hard to be a good influence.

"Burt," I pulled the cat away from his reach, "my dog Messy gets lonely, and I thought that if you don't mind, I'd adopt Legs." Now I was the big, fat liar. Messy would make sure I burned in hell for this hastily-conceived decision. Besides her general hatred of cats, Messy would never tolerate anything that might compete for her food bowl.

He took a minute and then said, "I'm not sure. I better call . . . "

My ears perked up. Who could he possibly have to call about the cat?

"I promise I'll take care of her." I walked the cat toward the door as if Burt had given me permission to take her. "Bye."

I raced to my rusty Honda Accord and drove quickly to Dr. Sherrod's where I left the trembling cat with Dr. Sherrod's terrific vet tech who assured me that Legs would be examined carefully and tenderly. I felt sure that Burt would leave the cat and me alone. He seemed more likely to bully than confront. Besides he was basically lazy, and pursuing Legs would require more energy than he could probably muster.

After the vet's, I returned to the office to make sure I'd left everything locked up. I poured a cup of coffee and felt pretty darn proud of myself. After all, I'd just spared Legs' life and would help find her a loving home—where that would be I wasn't sure.

I also wasn't sure what Scoop's saying *no* to alcohol would mean. I wanted his determination to last, but over the years, several bad hangovers had resulted in his swearing off demon rum for a week or so. The oath always wore off quickly, and he was once again closing every bar in a thirty-mile radius. I'd take a wait and see attitude.

Next, I allowed myself just one minute to think about Charley. A minute is all I could stand. I was in the throes of ingesting images of Charley's godlike self when he drove by in his gold, vintage Mercedes. Even in the darkness, I could see that next to him was an exquisitely beautiful blond. No matter how hard she tried to hide, Chloe Hite was immediately recognizable. She was his perfect match: beautiful, rich, and pampered, with one minor impediment: her marriage. Her husband Clarke Hite was older and the chief litigator for Cotter Manufacturing. *Not smart, Charley, dipping your pen in the company ink.* Forgive me, but at that moment, I was sick with envy. Chloe was sitting where I wanted to be.

But she could have him. I had bigger fish to fry and murders to investigate. Elli's house might have uncovered only a frightened cat, but someone somewhere knew the truth of what had happened to Elli and Mabel, and I intended to find who he or she was before the murderer found his next victim. Finding a murderer would keep me from wishing Charley could be better than he ever would be. Unexpectedly, I felt an overwhelming loss, telling myself it was because I missed Elli and felt bad about Mabel. It was only partly true.

Chapter Six

The next several days lulled me into the belief that a three-legged cat was the biggest problem I had. Murder actually took a backseat to finding Legs a home. Then it didn't. Another senseless death slapped me in the face. This one hit particularly close to home—if home is, indeed, where the heart is.

At first, though, I did think life in Cotter's Corner was returning to its safe predictability. The murderer had moved on, I told myself. Lacy perked up, once again living at her own house, resuming her relationship with Trey Davis, and looking pretty good--all things considered. The only downside was that she definitely was not in the market for a cat, three-legged or otherwise. Legs was mine—and Messy's.

Messy snarled whenever the cat came near so the timid feline figured out early that absence was the best policy. She steered clear of Messy. Since the vet's bill was astronomical, I'd already told myself that if Lacy didn't take Legs, I had to. She was nearly the biggest investment I'd made that year. So the undersized cat took up residence in the downstairs bedroom, on the bed, atop the polar fleece blanket, with pictures of dogs and cats, that I'd sewn for her. I should have been making quilt tops, and instead I spent my extra time making a real-life cat a home.

My peaceful, no-murders reverie was obliterated when my mother called and announced, out of the blue, that she was coming for the long-threatened visit. Since it was fall and a busy time for Chicago socialites, I smelled a rat. Or at least a Yates. I was betting that

Yates had her coming to plead on his behalf. That would be a cause as lost as finding a fourth leg for my cat. My mother and Scoop in the same town for longer than a weekend promised to be an invitation to disaster. But I was stuck.

I got hives. Big itchy ones that the doctor prescribed medicine for. They must have looked awful because even Scoop looked at the floor when he talked to me. All Lacy said when she saw my pathetic red spots was, "Your mother's coming, isn't she?" Fortunately the medicine the doctor prescribed nearly wiped away any trace of what my mother would zero in on as visible signs of my many imperfections.

I hadn't returned Charley's phone calls and got wind through the grapevine that he was in Europe on Cotter Foundation business, I bet. Monkey business was more like it, and his frisky frolicking companion was probably named Chloe. It was almost a relief to scratch him off my list of possible men. He was an impossible one.

Aggie was just leaving my house when my mother arrived. I was glad she didn't catch me alone. I would have time to decompress. My mother nearly took down two trees as she pulled into the driveway in the biggest Cadillac I'd ever seen.

"New car?" I asked as I kissed her and tried to keep myself from shaking all over. In her perfectly put-together, diminutive presence, my mother was a force to be reckoned with.

"Do you like it? I got it done yesterday." She patted her blindingly platinum hair. And she was Burberry from head to toe. I watched Aggie nervously straighten a pocket of her dreary flannel jacket, as if that would make her more presentable in my mother's critical eyes. I knew just how Aggie felt as I felt my mother's laser look pierce me from head to toe. Your jeans are worn out, your tee's too tight, she would think. And why do you shop at Kohl's? her disappointed eyes shouted. *This was going to be fun.*

"Looks like a suitcase display at Nordstrom's." Aggie tried to break the tension, which you couldn't cut with a chainsaw.

"How are you, Aggie, dear?" My mother can be such a phony.

"Fine, Cat; good to see you." Aggie doesn't have a phony bone in her body and showed it by using the nickname my mother absolutely hates because Scoop gave it to her when they first met.

The luggage! This was not going to be a short stay. My mother had packed as she does when she goes abroad with Leland. Yikes! "Are you going somewhere from here?" I asked hopefully, counting at least five very expensive suitcases.

My mother didn't answer. She was studying Aggie's flannel pants which were coated with hairs from her cat.

"Mother!" I snapped. "Are you going to answer my question, or are you going to rate our appearance?" It was no use. It took me all of four minutes to crack under the strain of being my mother's highly unsatisfying daughter.

She said nothing, but carried the two smallest pieces of luggage into my house. That left two for me and one for a more-gracious-than-my-mother-deserved Aggie.

I asked my question again. "Do you have another trip planned after this one?"

"Don't ask for plans!" My mother, who prides herself on always keeping an evenly-modulated tone, actually screamed. "I can't take it right now." To my shock, she came unglued before Aggie and me, right there in my hallway. Then she rushed into the living room and began frantically circling it. "What did I do to deserve this? My life is over! I'm lost." She was scaring me.

I would have put my arm around her if she'd stayed still. "What's wrong, Mother? Are you sick?"

"No! I'm not sick. I'm not sick! I'm over fifty!"

"You're this upset over getting older?" I felt the blood rushing to my cheeks. I knew she was a vain woman, but this was absurd, and embarrassing. "You're throwing a fit because you're aging?"

"No, it's not about my age. It's worse." She wrung her hands and paced back and forth.

"You're poor?" That was the only thing I could think that would affect my mother more than aging. "That's what it is, right? Leland has made bad investments. You don't have to worry. I have all that money he's given me and this house, too. He bought this house. You and he can have it all back." My mother was a mess, and I felt an urgency to help her.

"Oh, Samuels, don't be dense. I'm not sick, and I'm not poor. I'm getting a divorce. Leland wants to marry someone else."

I never saw it coming. I knew their marriage was a travesty on many levels, but I never saw her leaving him and, more unfathomable, him leaving her. Being rid of Leland would be far from the worst thing in my life, but I knew it would be terrible for my mother. For nearly twenty years, being Mrs. Leland Henry of Chicago, Palm Beach, and Oahu had defined her.

"If he's found some young idiot who's impressed by his money, you're better off without him." It was the best I could come up with.

"She's not that young and she's no idiot. She's a judge, soon to be a state supreme court judge. Oh, I knew I should have gotten that law degree!" My mother sobbed and sobbed and sobbed and sobbed.

When I couldn't take it anymore, I took another tack. "Well, the worst has happened and you're still standing. And you're going to stay here. I want you here." I was having an out-of-body experience.

"You haven't heard the worst yet." She hadn't paid any attention to my magnanimous gesture. Maybe I could pretend I'd never offered. My mother ranted on, "She has a three-year-old, Leland's three-year-old. How will I ever live with the shame! And the little boy's name is Thurgood. Who names a child Thurgood? His nickname will be Thurg, for God's sake! They'll make mincemeat of that kid on the playground!"

"Right. That kid has bigger problems than we have," I laughed. My mother didn't. "Well, the woman's a judge. Obviously she's black and admires Thurgood Marshall."

"She's lily white, and her son is lily-white and red-headed. I know because he was there, with her, when Leland told me he was leaving me. They've been carrying on for four years!" Tears, tears, and more tears.

"Mother." I knelt in front of her, picking up the Kleenex she was throwing to the floor as she finished weeping into them. "You've known there were other women. This can't be that great a shock."

"It's a terrible shock. Yes, I knew there were other women from time to time, but there were a lot of them. They left as quickly as they came. This one stayed. She isn't one of his silly women. She's smart and goal-oriented. And she's crafty. Truthfully, she's a lot like me." My mother paused as if to consider the truth of what she'd just said. "I thought he respected me and would always want me to be his wife. He doesn't respect me at all." The last several words were buried in her tortured sobs. If she'd cried like this all the way from Chicago, she was lucky to be alive.

"Cat!" Aggie's loud voice bounced off the walls. "Pull yourself together, young lady! You and I both know that you've been in tougher spots than this."

Total silence.

Then my mother said, "I'm sorry, Aggie." My mother was positively penitent.

"Don't be sorry," Aggie commanded, "be the Cat I know. Be the Cat I watched take off into a blinding snowstorm to the drugstore so she could get medicine for her sick little girl. I want you to be the Cat who left this town with five hundred dollars and a two-and-a half-year-old child in tow. That Cat saved herself and her little girl. Now you call her back right this minute."

"Oh, Aggie!" The next thing I knew, my mother was laughing, crying, and hugging Aggie.

"Okay. Okay." Aggie patted her and then said, "Now get down off that high horse and start putting your life back together. Welcome home, Cat."

Instead of recoiling, which I was sure she would, my mother leaned into Aggie, little girl-like. "I'm going to stay here. I think I've been homesick for a long time."

My mother was resolute. I was dead. How could I have her around twenty-four/seven? I'd have to find someplace else to live. Maybe with Aggie?

"You look positively panic stricken," my mother wiped away tears and laughed. "I don't mean I'm going to live here. Not here in your house. No offense, pet, but it's far too small. I mean I'm going to find a place around here. There's no need to ever go back to Chicago. I'll send for my things."

"Grand Rapids is close," I stammered, "and it's a bigger city. You love big cities. Remember how much you loved Chicago? And Grand Rapids has good theatre and a great symphony orchestra!"

"Not really. I'm a small town girl at heart, aren't I, Aggie?"

Aggie, too, looked as if having my mother around full-time might be more than she was ready for. "Well, you did get tired of it." Aggie said hesitantly, not wanting to set my mother off again.

"I got tired of Scoop. Without him, I would have been very happy here."

"But he's still here," I said to my mother who was just not hearing me.

I watched as my mother recreated herself before our eyes. She was doing what she did when she became Leland Henry's wife. I wondered if she even knew who she really was. I sure didn't.

"But . . . " I couldn't think of what should come next.

"No 'but'. I'm staying and that's that." She took a drink of the latté I'd made for her. I really am good with that little espresso machine.

I made one last ditch effort. "You're upset. Let's get you settled. You'll think more clearly then."

"I couldn't be thinking any more clearly than I am. I've thought about Cotter's Corner all the way from Chicago. It was my home once, and it's going to be again." She squeezed a stunned-looking Aggie's hand.

"Just remember," I spoke in a sing-song voice, "you always said Chicago is your kind of town."

"Was," she corrected. "It *was* my kind of town. I loved being Mrs. Leland Henry," she took out a mirror and made a face at the face that stared back, and reapplied her lip gloss. "That makes me sound shallow, huh? Well, I was. We all do what we need to do to survive." She squared her shoulders as if she defied me to challenge her logic. *Not me.*

I sighed. I had no energy left to debate what I felt deep down was a very bad idea, for both of us.

"What's that?!" My mother jumped from the chair she'd collapsed into only a few moments before. "Oh, look at that dreadful thing."

"It's a cat, Mother. Calm down." I picked up Legs. "It belonged to one of the murder victims. Nobody wanted her. This is a very dangerous place to live, you know." I couldn't believe I hadn't played the murder card. I was slipping.

"Then, we have something in common, don't we kitty?" My mother took Legs from me and gently scratched her ears. Legs purred like there was no tomorrow. "We've both been displaced—or in my case—replaced." For a second, my mother looked as if she was going to burst into tears again, but she looked at Aggie and hugged Legs to her. "I guess you're a little cute. Look at those darling markings around your eyes. It looks like you have eye liner on." Legs studied her as if trying to understand what she said. I looked at my mother as if she'd gone totally bonkers.

"She's had quite a time of it," I said. "I took her to the vet to have her checked over and spent a small fortune."

I expected my mother to ream me for spending money on a homeless, homely stray cat, but instead she cradled Legs and drank more of the latté. "She likes me, doesn't she?"

Ordinarily, I would have pointed out to my mother that I was sure with Legs it was any port in a storm, but I felt too sorry for both of them to throw a cold bucket of reality onto their shared suffering.

After a supper of hot chicken salad, delivered in warp speed by Lacy, and three jumbo tumblers of wine, my mother was safely sleeping in the guest bedroom, or Legs' bedroom as I now thought of it. Legs, of course, slept practically on top of her head.

"You'll get through this," Aggie put her hands on my shoulders as she went to get her coat from the closet. "We'll get through this," she muttered as she opened the door of her crumbling pickup parked behind my mother's leviathan Caddy.

"Yeah," I said into the cold night air as she drove away. "I hope so."

Finally, I was alone. I made a list of things to pick up at The Ample Spoon, our haute cuisine deli half a block from The Corner News. Next I poured yet another glass of wine and plopped onto the sofa to watch the DVD of *Downton Abbey*, *Season Two*. Messy slept next to me. This is living, isn't it girl? Mommy will go to the deli in a little while, once she has sobered up."

The food would have to wait. Within minutes, I was asleep next to a snoring Messy. The doorbell woke me up. It startled me so that I had that queasy stomach feeling you get sometimes when you're too quickly roused.

"Just thought I'd stop by. Hey, looks like you just got out of bed." Scoop looked around the room as he entered. "Noticed you have company. I saw her broom parked in your driveway."

"She's sleeping," I spoke in a low tone hoping he'd take the hint. "We both were. Hey, let me tell you about that little device you use to troll for dates. It's called a phone and is very useful in moments like this."

"Well, sorrrrrrrrrrrrrry. Someone sure woke up on the wrong side of the sofa. I was just checking to make sure the two of you hadn't killed each other yet."

"Listen, it's you and Mother who can't stand each other. She and I get along just fine."

"And you're living in Cotter's Corner because . . .?"

"Because I wanted a change and because I make very bad decisions. Anything else?"

I could tell he was winding up to say something that would really set me off, but he stopped mid-breath.

"Hello, Harley," my mother waltzed into the room.

"Cat," he nodded, "I was just telling our daughter that I noticed you parked your weapon of mass destruction in her driveway."

"Scoop! Enough! Mother's going through a bit of a difficult time." I'd totally had it with the Bickersons.

"Not another word, Samuels." My mother was absolutely regal. It was her "I'll rise above this" pose.

"Trouble in paradise?" he asked unsympathetically.

"It looks like her marriage is over," I shot back. "Are you happy now? She's thinking about moving here."

"My God," he said, "the world as I know it has ended. Shoot me. Shoot me now."

My mother walked over and stood nose to nose with him. "If I only had a gun."

"If you only had a Tic Tac," he smirked. "How much did you drink?"

"Pig! How about putting that banana-shaped ego of yours aside? Remember that we were once married and that I might deserve an ounce of concern." She was at her dramatic best.

"An ounce, but not a bit more." He was his most smartass self.

"Okay." I hoped that he would take the cue to leave, but he was cueless.

"Sorry, Cat," Scoop walked toward her, but she stepped back, signaling another step forward might put his life in his hands. "I came here to give you some news." He turned to me.

"Give." I said, pretty fed up with both of them.

"Charles Cotter Senior." That was all he said.

"I'm not kidding, Scoop. I'm tired, and I'm mean. What do you know about Charley's dad."

"Dad dead." He said and waited for both my mother and me to react.

"Do you mean that awful Charley's dad, who owns this town?" My mother asked.

"The very one. Trey Davis stopped in to tell me when he was on his way back to the police station. Someone found Charles Cotter at his desk at The Cotter Foundation. There's no doubt that it was suicide. I guess he blew his brains out."

My mother and I both recoiled at the image.

"Poor Charley." I was sick for him and for the town both. Another unexplained death.

"He was always a pretty depressed guy." Scoop said. "There's no doubt about it. He was a puzzle, but there's also no question that he did a ton for this town."

"Why? Why would he do this to his son?" I couldn't imagine how Charley would take the news. They were a notoriously distant father and son, but they were still father and son. "They had such a complicated relationship."

"Not that complicated," Scoop snorted. "The old man gave his kid everything but attention. Anytime they were together, you'd never guess they were father and son. The truth is that Charley's dad never got over that accident that killed his wife."

"Accident?" My mother was all ears.

"Happened when Charley was about five. He and his mother were passengers in a car that Charles Senior was driving. He lost control on black ice and the car hit a tree. Mrs. Cotter was the only one seriously injured. She lived for a long time but was pretty much out of it. She died in a rehab center when Charley was in his early teens."

"I never knew," I said.

"I'm not sure how many people knew. Like I said. Cotter Senior was a puzzle."

"And now he's dead." My mother said. "How sad."

"Maybe I should go over there to see how Charley's doing." I was thinking aloud.

"Listen, Missy," Scoop's eyes became lasers, "stay out of it. Charley Cotter will be just fine. When did you not know that golden boy to land on his feet?"

"For once, I agree with your father, Sam." My mother put a hand on my shoulder. "Charley Cotter's business is none of yours."

"Besides," Scoop added, "Trey said that when he went to tell Charley that his father was dead, some nubile nymph answered the door. Probably Chloe Hite. She's chased him ever since she got married. And word is that way too many times she's caught him."

Scoop went to the newspaper; I left my mother in front of the television watching HBO and drinking tea, Legs lying next to her. I headed toward the deli to buy food so my refrigerator would house something besides my staples of cheese, crackers, celery, and carrots.

But I couldn't help myself. Before I went to get the food, I drove by Charley's. I told myself I wanted to make sure he wasn't alone, but I was also curious as to whether or not Chloe's Jaguar would be parked in the driveway. It was, along with half a dozen other cars. Scoop was right. Charley was being well cared for.

"Did you hear about Mr. Cotter?" Annette Stancati, the owner of The Ample Spoon, practically attacked me the minute I walked in the door. She flashed both her signature smile and her eagerness to share the latest gossip. "Isn't it awful?"

"My dad told me about it just a little while ago." I pointed toward the chicken salad.

"Mr. Cotter was sure good to this town, but not very friendly." Annette scooped up the chicken salad and then headed to the three-bean salad, lasagna, honey wheat bread, ambrosia and tiramisu that I also ordered.

"I didn't know him, not really," I said. "Can I have some of those brownies, too?" I knew they were a favorite of my mother's. "Oh, and I need a quart of your unsweetened raspberry iced tea."

"How's Charley?" Annette was determined to stay on the subject that I was eager to avoid.

"Trey said he's doing about as well as can be expected." I grabbed up the food so I could get out of there. "Oops. I forgot soup. Could you scoop up a couple quarts each of sauterne mushroom and red pepper vegetable?" My mother loved those, too.

"Sure." She talked as she scooped. "You know that Chloe Hite and Charley have kind of a thing, right? She's always been crazy about him. Don't blame her. I went out with him a couple of times one summer. He's hot." Annette had drifted back to a different time, different place. I too had a vivid, sensual recollection of a certain time and place.

"She's married, though."

"Yeah, right, married. Some husbands don't have a clue. But then, word is that her husband is so crazy about her he'll put up with anything. Boy, Jimmy would knock me from here to tomorrow if I did that." Annette referred to her trucker husband Jimmy Stancati—one of the three brawling Stancati brothers. Jimmy had been Mr. Everything in high school and Mr. Nobody after that. Word was that Annette did get knocked around by her all brawn and no heart spouse.

"Maybe I'll take some food over there." She said it as if she were asking a question.

"That's nice." *Not so nice, though, if her husband Jimmy caught her cozying up to her former heartthrob.*

I paid for the food and began to leave.

"At least it wasn't murder, huh? When I first heard, I was sure it was another murder. It gave me the creeps. I mean, what would this town do if it had another murder?" I was at the door and Annette was still chattering.

"I don't know." I left, tired of the conversation.

It was dark so I unlocked my car and quickly got inside. My mind was on the conversation with Annette. No matter how you spun it, his father's death would be devastating for Charley and for Cotter's Corner too.

My house was only blocks away, but about halfway home, I saw that a car behind me was rapidly gaining on me. I hadn't noticed it earlier because it had no front headlights. Then it was next to me, forcing me to turn quickly and irresponsibly to the right. I went up on the sidewalk, narrowly missing a light pole. The car behind me stopped for a second before accelerating and racing by. I was breathless and weak. Ordinarily, I would have blamed my near accident on reckless teens out for a good time. But good times in Cotter's Corner had been few and far between lately. This was not kids. This was no accident.

I eased my car back onto the road and drove home. Once in my driveway, I dialed Lacy. "Is Trey there?"

"Sure. I'll get him. Are you all right? You sound strange."

"Someone tried to run me off the road. I need to talk to Trey about it."

"What's up?" he asked, sounding as if he didn't give a darn.

"When I was driving home from the deli, a car tried to run me off the road."

"Now, Sam, I know things have been scary lately, but we can't let every little thing lead us to think the boogie man is out to get us."

Damn him. I knew calling him would be a big mistake. "Bye." I threw the phone on the seat next to mine. How could my beautiful, loving friend be tied up with such a total creep? Trey Davis had been a high school badass. Now he was just an ass.

Once inside my house, in order to survive the chain collision of thoughts ramming my brain, I pulled my mental trick of thinking only about the present. The present was Messy, Legs, and my mother—who sat for who knew how long on my sofa watching TV. The present was also Charley, his father's suicide, and, of course, those darn unsolved murders.

Chapter Seven

Cats are nothing if they aren't unpredictable. During the next day or so, Legs fell totally in love with my mother. The timid cat curled at her feet and purred against her whenever she got the chance. And though I'd never known Catherine Hayes Henry to be at ease among even the safest and sweetest of animals, with the three-legged cat, she was both gentle and adoring. This was very good for Legs because Messy hated her. She growled whenever the cat was as close as two rooms away and seemed to resent every hair of Legs' furry self.

Totally predictable? That would be Trey Davis. The two calls I'd made to the police station to see if there had been any follow-up to my car being forced off the road were greeted with Trey's snotty, nonplused response. "Chill, Sam. I'm telling you that kids will be kids."

And jerks will be jerks.

I confess to pathetically little mind control where Charley was concerned. I listened carefully whenever someone mentioned him, and nearly stumbled over a cookie display in the grocery store when I overheard a woman in the next line saying something about Charley. I ended up purchasing four packages of damaged Oreos and gaining no information where he of the luscious body and golden locks was concerned.

However, I garnered from my friend Lacy, also Charley's friend, that he had taken over the manufacturing plant as if he'd always been there. Days passed and all I heard regarding the senior Cotter's death was that the funeral was large and private. I hadn't been invited.

"What did I ever do without Aggie?" my mother asked a couple of days after the suicide and a couple of weeks before Thanksgiving. I'd given little thought to the holiday for obvious reasons. "She has found me a wonderful realtor and is going along as I look at houses today." I survived by telling myself that my mother would never find a house that would meet her demands. "When your father was off being his awful self," she continued, "Aggie took you off my hands so I could go shopping for fabric or groceries. He just was not around. Did I ever tell you that?"

"So you've said." *Again and again and again.* "I think you and Scoop are hugely different, and that was a large part of the problem."

"Aggie is just like your Aunt Cathy." My mother ignored the Scoop part of my conversation. "I don't know why I didn't see it before."

"For a long time, you didn't see anything good about anyone here." I reminded her.

"Did I tell you that Aggie and Hilda are in a sewing group? They sew things for churches and charity. Isn't that nice?"

"Look," I pulled the basket of half-made quilt tops from under the table, "these are what I've been talking about—for years!"

"Would you mind if I took Legs with me?" It was out of the blue and a total non sequitur.

"Where?"

"When I get my new house, of course. Do you mind giving Legs to me? I've come to love her so much?" My mother actually batted her eyes. Messy stood at attention.

I was flabbergasted. "I guess. She does seem to like you."

"I know. Babies and animals never like me, and yet Leggs seems to adore me."

"Then, what better reason to adopt a pet!"

"Thank you! I have a house I'm looking at, and if it works, I'll be moving in a week or so."

"That soon?" I tried to tamp down the jubilation coursing through me. "What house?" *Please oh please don't let it be next door.*

"I can't say just yet. It might not work out, but if it does, it will be perfect. I'll know in a day or two. I'll tell you as soon as I know for sure."

"You're sure you can afford it?" I hadn't gotten into discussions of money since my mother's breakdown in the living room. "Oh, yes. Leland really wants to be rid of me quickly. He's giving me more than the assets of some third world country."

As I'd expected, all talk of quilts was gone. For the next few days my mother was up to her ears in phone calls and business meetings. "It's a done deal," she announced the week before Thanksgiving. "I got the house! Let's have Thanksgiving there."

"Where?" I crossed my fingers and toes. Since I hadn't seen a "Sold" sign go up on my street, I felt fairly safe. "I'm happy you have the house, but you'll have to get your things out of storage. Thanksgiving on top of all that might be too much, don't you think?"

"I'm moving tomorrow. I bought it fully furnished and will worry about changing things later."

I was starting to get a glimmer of what I thought would not be a good idea. "Whose house did you buy?"

"Charles Cotter's."

My heart sank. Charley was moving. "Charley's?"

"Not Charley's. His father's house next door. I've been negotiating with the estate and we waited for Charley to return from a business trip to finalize the agreement."

"You're going to live next door to Charley?" I suddenly envied my mother. *Tell Chloe hello for me,* I thought.

"We signed the papers early today. It's perfect. I'm even keeping the housekeeper who, according to Charley, is a gem."

"So you and Charley are on speaking terms?"

"I must say, he's been very fair. I thought I was going to have to pay a lot more. It's a gorgeous house, done in perfect taste. I can move in as is, though I probably will have to make changes later."

My mother wasn't kidding about how fast she was moving. Within twenty-four hours, she was gone. Her divorce wasn't final, but Leland had obviously been willing to give her everything her vengeful little heart desired to get rid of her. Leggs left with my mother, along with the new Louis Vuitton duffle she'd bought for the cat and a raft of newly-acquired playthings.

"It's just you and me, Messy." I ate some leftover chicken salad, cold, and pulled out the old Singer. It was either think about death or sewing. I chose the latter and got busy on the quilt squares that had been waiting patiently for me.

The phone rang.

"Charley wants to take us out to celebrate—at the country club. He's already put me up for membership." My mother's voice was ecstatic. It would be a victory for her to belong to the country club in a town she'd left under cover of darkness. I feared it would signal the return of imperious Catherine Henry. And I dreaded looking at Charley's duplicitous face.

"You two are getting pretty friendly." I stalled for time and a good excuse.

"It's business. But he's making an effort to be friendly so how can we say 'no'?"

The way I felt about meeting Charley at his club defined ambivalent. I wanted to see him, be near him. I also wanted to avoid him because I knew he promised temporary ecstasy and long-term suffering.

In my life, I've probably been at The Cotter's Corner Country Club half a dozen times, mostly when Leland and my mother came to visit and he used his country club visitors' exchange. Going with Charley was a whole new experience.

First, no one could take his or her eyes off him when we walked in. I, too, thought he was captivating in a camel jacket and dark slacks. Though I think I looked pretty fetching in my LBD, I was put on alert by Charley's attention to my mother and almost total ignoring of her daughter. He even had my mother giggling and having her champagne glass filled again and again. Toward me, he was frosty at best.

"Your mother and I are neighbors. Does that mean that I'll be seeing you a lot in the neighborhood?" He swirled his drink. He didn't make it sound as if it was something he looked forward to.

"Probably a little," I said. He wasn't the only one who could play reluctant and aloof.

"I see someone I know from Chicago," my mother pointed toward a table across the room. "I'll be back in a little while." But she left and didn't head to the designated table.

"I think she wants to leave us alone," Charley said.

"I can't understand why. I thought the whole point of this was to celebrate your being neighbors."

"Okay." He was angry. "I don't know what has changed you so suddenly, but how about letting me in on it so it's a fair playing field? I have done everything to get your attention including selling my dad's house at a way too good bargain price."

"Charley, for a very brief moment or two, I considered going out with you, as you said to see what lies between us. Then you and Chloe drove by and it was cold water thrown on my face."

"So that's why you didn't call when my dad died? That hurt, Sam."

"I sent you a card, a pretty card, and I thought about dropping in, but the lustrous Chloe beat me to it."

"So I have baggage, sometimes clinging baggage, but I'm trying to work through my bad habits."

"By keeping them up?" I saw my mother walking back, very slowly.

"I broke it off with Chloe. But you can't throw someone out of your car, when she runs up to it saying she's getting a divorce, or when she shows up when you've suffered a massive personal tragedy. You made your decision about me without taking the time to see if you were right or not."

"They weren't the people I thought they were," my mother said as Charley made a hasty retreat. "What's up?"

"He had to go to the men's room. You left to let me and Charley talk, didn't you? I don't get it. For years you've hated him and now because you get a great deal on a house, you're his bestie."

"That's not true. I saw a different Charley when I dealt with him over the house. And then when he called to ask if we couldn't go to dinner so he could talk to you, it didn't seem like a bad idea."

"You'll never learn." I slammed my napkin down on the table.

"Where are you going?"

"Where I should have stayed. Home!"

It wasn't one of my best ideas. No moon out. Very dark, and very cold and slippery in my heels. The black dress's matching jacket was warm, but it covered very little. One block away from the club and a half a dozen blocks to go, I was frozen. I was also scared. I thought about turning back, but I had too much pride.

"Ride?" Charley's Mercedes pulled alongside. "You can be proud or you can be smart."

"Where's my mother?" I climbed in beside him.

"She called Scoop and they're going to share what would have been a wonderful meal."

"Charley, I might as well say it, I think I was looking for an excuse to stop something before it started. You scare me."

"You scare me more," he gently stroked the side of my face before pulling me to him. "I don't know what to do with you, never have."

"Then why start?" He was kissing me. I was kissing him.

"Because I find you irresistible." He kissed my neck. Then he kissed me again. "I remember that kiss." Then I was lost in a sea of kisses, long and demanding. Charley was a masterful kisser.

I pulled away. "And Chloe and all those other Chloes?"

"I may have to spend years convincing you, but the events of the past few weeks have forced me to grow up. I'm now the head of the family, only I don't have a family."

"I remember those kisses, too." I kissed him back, slowly and deliberately.

"So are we settled? Do you think we can have a date now?" He stroked my cheek.

"I think so." Good decision or bad decision, it was the decision I made. "But how do you think Chloe will feel when she hears we're going out?" I was only half teasing. Chloe Hite thought Charley was hers. How *would* she feel?

He stopped his car in front of my house. "I told you that Chloe and I are done. She's just having a hard time getting used to the idea." He nuzzled my neck as he spoke.

"I'm too easy," I said as I began to open my door. "I gave in too quickly."

He looked at me. "Are you kidding? You easy? Sam, you couldn't be making this more difficult. And from the beginning I knew you couldn't be a casual fling. You're not the girl to fool around with. Never have been."

"Why me? Charley, whenever I think about the two of us together, I get to the part where we break up and I'm left full of regret and heartbreak."

"Talk about being a cup half empty person. Did you ever think we might be perfect for each other? That's what I've been wondering. I look at you," he was at my door, helping me from the car "and what I see is a smart, beautiful woman who's never and will never put up with my shit. My dad's death really did change my thinking. He let someone get away and was forever lost. I don't want to be that guy, Sam."

I wanted Charley to stay, oh how I wanted Charley to stay, but one more kiss and I sent him on his way. I was patting Messy when my cell rang.

"Hi, Sam, I just wanted to make sure that you got home safely and you're not mad at me."

"It's fine, Mother. I'm fine."

"Then I'll let you go," she giggled and then I heard another, all-too-familiar laugh."

"Goodbye." I said.

If my decision to date Charley was a bad decision, my Mother's decision to hang with Scoop was worse. *Please don't let me be my mother's daughter.*

Chapter Eight

Lacy had a new boyfriend. Being Lacy she didn't talk much about him, but it was clear that she and Luke Barrett, fairly new to town and the owner of The Barrett insurance Agency were an item. I surmised he might be the mysterious man she'd intended to meet for drinks the night her aunt was murdered. He hadn't grown up in Cotter's Corner, so I didn't know him, but from the little I did know, he seemed a whole lot better than Trey. She spilled the beans one day when I was having lunch with her at Mabel's.

"How does Trey feel about your dating Luke?" I asked.

"Doesn't matter. Trey and I are through. It's no business of his who I date." She was uncharacteristically dismissive. "Besides, he has someone on the side. I've known about it for a while. When I'd ask him, he'd tell me I was crazy. But he came home one night reeking of perfume that's definitely not mine. I sent him packing."

"Good." I hoped she meant to keep him gone.

"Now you can tell me any time about how right I was where you and Charley are concerned," she smiled wickedly.

"Don't get too smug. We're taking it very slowly."

"All I'll say is that I've known you both for a long time, and I don't remember ever seeing either of you happier."

"He is pretty wonderful," I said in a totally unguarded moment. "I had such a different opinion of him, but he's caring and loving."

"And your mother?" Lacy laughed. "Somehow I can't imagine either of your parents is that happy about you and Charley 'keeping company,' as they say."

"My mother is grateful to Charley for the house and so buried in redecorating and her sewing group that she hasn't paid much attention to me. And she did invite him for Thanksgiving, even though the new range she ordered was delayed and he had to end up taking us to his club. As for Scoop, he's not a bit happy. And I'm not happy that he's following my mother around in a kind of creepy puppy dog way so I'm off his radar, too."

"Then you know what I say? Have fun, girl!"

"Turn about is fair play. Tell me when you hooked with Luke?"

"Not long ago. And I don't know how long it will last. We're really different, but he's a nice guy. We'll see."

Charley dropped in at the paper after I'd seen Lacy.

"Do you mind my dropping in?"

He knew I didn't. "What's up?"

"Luke Barrett just called and wants to double with you and me. I told him I'd get back to him."

"Sure," I said. That's how the four of us wound up at a Matt Damon thriller the next night. I could immediately see what Lacy meant. There was no chemistry between them. Luke is clean-cut and well-dressed but stiff. Lacy's more fun. She spent the evening kidding Charley and me. I felt bad that I couldn't see Luke and her lasting more than a few more dates.

Charley left his car in front of my house so that Luke could drive. On the way home, we grabbed coffee and pie. Then the evening was definitely and happily, I'm sorry to say, almost over.

"Don't get spooked," Luke said when he was two blocks from my house, "but someone is coming up on us pretty fast."

Charley pulled his arm from around me and looked out the window. "What the hell?!"

"Call the police," Lacy told Charley when the car threatened to try to pass us on a narrow residential street. "Who is that? I don't recognize the car."

"Don't call the police," Luke commanded. "I know who it is and they're not out to hurt us. Someone is mad at me."

"*You*?" Charley continued to dial.

"I'm serious, Charley. Don't call. I'll take care of it. See? The car is backing off. And look here. We're home."

"Luke, I can't believe you didn't do something about this," Lacy's voice registered her fear.

"Perhaps it wouldn't have been the smartest thing to call the police considering we'd probably get your ex." Charley tried to relieve the tension.

"Sam, do you mind if I stay with you tonight?" Lacy nearly leapt from the car. "Luke, I don't need a ride home," she said before I answered her question.

"Goodnight," Luke said and drove off leaving the three of us standing in front of my house confused.

"I can't believe I thought he was a nice guy," Lacy said. "Goes to show you that I don't know shit about men."

"Hey," Charley put his arms around both of us as we walked inside, "we don't know that he's still not a nice guy, just a little weird." We laughed.

"I was wondering," Charley whispered to me as I unlocked the door, "if you'd mind if I stayed overnight, too." That's how it happened. Lacy stayed upstairs and

Charley and I slept downstairs, though we didn't get much sleep.

I heard Lacy leave early the next morning for the restaurant. That would have left Charley and me with lots of time to stay in bed and explore every part of each other if my mother hadn't rung the doorbell. I slipped out of bed, leaving Charley deep in sleep.

"Mother, it's so early!" I wrapped the robe around me and hoped Charley didn't come trotting down the stairs.

"I wanted you to know that I'm really and truly and finally divorced. The papers came by registered mail a little while ago. Leland got a quickie in the Caribbean."

"Are you sad?" I ushered her into the kitchen where I would endeavor to get past my love-drunk fog to make some lattés for us.

"I'm not. And I'm surprised I'm not," she said as she took off her coat. "Oh, there was a time I loved Leland, not a great love, but it was love. He was good to me and certainly gave you and me everything we wanted. But that was over after I learned about his first airhead. And when he asked for a divorce, I was stunned more than heartbroken. Let's face it. It's never fun to be replaced. Now, though, I feel free. I don't know if I've ever in my life been this free." Her eyes glistened.

"I do have one concern," I said. "Dad's kind of worming his way back into your life."

"Not really. Your father and I had something very powerful, and I'm sure there's a little of that left."

"Oh, my gosh, you wouldn't go back to him!"

Her face registered terror. "Oh no! Never! But he is a little sexy, and he can be charming. And we do share this wonderful young woman. It's nice that we're not constantly at each other's throats, don't you think?"

"Just don't let him be your rebound guy." Now I was the parent.

"Don't worry. I'm in control this time, and it's damn fun! Now how about that coffee?"

I'd poured her a cup and was pouring mine when a half-dressed Charley walked into the kitchen and came face to face with my mother.

"I can't believe you're lecturing me. Look what you've been up to. Well, aren't I the little matchmaker."

If I lived to be a thousand, I would never understand my mother.

"It's my fault, Mrs. Henry. We had a bit of a scare last night, and I stayed over to make sure she was safe."

"Oh, I see."

"It's true," I said. "Lacy was here, too, but she had to go to work. Honest." It *was* partially true.

"Charley, you are charming, but you are a scamp." She couldn't keep herself from smiling. "You'd better not hurt my girl."

"Never." He took the cup of coffee I handed him and kissed me right on the lips, right in front of my mother.

Perfect timing. The man we'd both been known to refer to as our worst nightmare walked in the door, again without ringing the bell.

"Coffee! Great!" He entered without an apology for entering. "Hi, Cat. I saw your car."

"You don't knock, Harley?" My mother was probably concerned Scoop might have heard more than she wanted him to.

"You will feel so bad when you find out why I've come—to spare your finding out the news somewhere else."

The air went out of my love balloon. "More bad news?" I knew the answer before I finished asking the question.

"Burt Lundy was found behind Elli's work shed. Somebody bashed his head in. Judging from the condition of the body, he'd probably been there for days. Moe probably thought nothing of his being absent from work a few days because Burt was known for taking days off to drink."

"I wish I could muster some sympathy. He was such a douche!" I said without thinking.

"Samuels," my mother shook her finger at me disapprovingly.

"Miss Hayes!" Charley winked approvingly.

"Who is this Burt Lundy?" My mother had regained her composure and her curiosity.

"He wasn't living here when you were, Cat. By then he'd been shipped off to his first stint in prison. From then on, he was an intermittent guest. A born loser, no doubt about it. Mr. Cotter," he turned to Charley, "I'm dumbfounded as to why you'd be here so early in the morning."

"We had a car chase us home," I felt like I was fifteen, "so Charley stayed to keep Lacy and me company."

"Kinky." My dad was boring a hole through Charley.

"Harley! Must you always be uncouth and vulgar."

"Hope so," he said. "Now back to you, Mr. Cotter."

"I told you that—"

"Sam, I'm talking to Charley and he knows why I'm talking to him."

"That I do, Scoop, but I promise I am not taking your daughter casually. Anyone who knows Sam knows that's not possible."

"So that's how you feel today. But the trouble is that Sam is *my* daughter, and I need to know that tomorrow I won't see you with one of your other Cotter's Corner women. You know what and whom I'm talking about."

"Harley, leave it alone." My mother, surprise of all surprises, stepped in. "Charley and Sam are adults. We have no right to get into their business."

Charley's and my business was exactly what *she'd* been into minutes before my dad arrived, but I wasn't about to remind her. Instead I mentally thanked her for the cease fire and poured some coffee for Scoop.

"Where are the police? Scoop, you said you'd talked to the state police. This is a small town. I can't believe someone doesn't have some answers. It's been weeks, hasn't it?" My mother was struggling valiantly to change the subject.

"There are too many leads but none of them solid."

Now it was Aggie's turn to blast through the door and appear in my kitchen. "Hear you nearly got run off the road last night?"

"How did you know?" Charley asked.

"Scanner." My mother, father, and I said in unison.

"Scanner," Aggie confirmed. "One of your neighbors saw the whole thing, but couldn't get the license plate and didn't recognize the car."

"It was someone Luke Barrett knows," I told them. "Charley was dialing the police, but Luke didn't want him to call. He said he'd handle it."

"Hope not like he did last night." Aggie took something from my cupboard to pour into her coffee, and it wasn't cream. "That could have been serious."

"She's right." My mother wilted. "I'm starting to think that I've bought a house in a Stephen King novel."

"Hey, Cat," my dad pounced on my mother's vulnerability, "how about if I pull a Charley and stay in that big, beautiful house of yours to protect you. I'm great at protecting. Over and over and over."

Charley laughed; I tried to keep from gagging, and my mother became a blaze of fury.

"You don't actually think I would ever let you— protect—me again!"

"Don't flatter yourself," he looked a bit humiliated. "I just meant if you need someone to sleep on the couch, I'm available."

"So is a rent-a-cop," she said, "and they come with less baggage."

Maybe I'd misread the giggling the night my mother called. I hoped so.

"On that note," Scoop pushed his chair away and rose, "I'm going to work. Let you know if I find out more about Burt." He didn't say goodbye.

"I think I was too harsh," my mother said as her eyes followed Scoop out the door.

"He deserved it. And he'll recover." He deserved that and more I told myself.

"I'd better get to work, too." Charley tucked his shirt in his pants.

"Thanks so much for my house, Charley." She left.

"Alone." I put my arms around him.

"At last." His kiss was warm, loving, and restrained.

"You all right?" I searched his face for answers.

"I am, but I want you to be. Your parents have a point, you know. I'm the bad boy of this and many other towns and college campuses. You might regret it if we get in any deeper."

"I was in very deep one night, and as I recall, you pulled me out of the water and saved my life. I don't think you'll hurt me."

"I'll do my damndest not to." With those words, I would have kissed him for the rest of my life if Messy hadn't wound around us begging to go out.

"It's Saturday. How about if I make us something tonight? Or, more likely, I will probably order pizza and salads. How's that?"

"That, you hot, hot girl, would be perfect. I'll bring the wine." One more kiss and he left.

What a morning, I thought, as I put the coffee cups in the dishwasher.

Saturday morning. There was no urgency about getting to the paper, no need to do anything except think of the marathon, Richter Scale-rocking night I'd had with Charley. I cared for him, and I knew that was putting me in dangerous territory.

Burt Lundy was dead, murdered. Violently. Brutally, Painfully. I knew it without the information provided by Aggie's scanner. I knew it without the news that blared away on my kitchen television. The murder was ghastly.

But at last there was a connection! The murderer, who'd been so smart up to now, might be getting cocky. Burt and Elli were related. Maybe the police would be able to unearth a reason they were singled out by their attacker. Maybe. I didn't know how Mabel fit in, but I felt there was something about Burt's death that might help answer who killed her, too.

"Guess what!" Even on the phone, I could tell Lacy was smiling. "Trey's back. He was here when I got home from working the breakfast shift. We had such a serious, wonderful talk, and I totally misread him. He had an extra job. That's why he was so busy. He was working as a mall cop. That job is over. He's moving back in."

"Lacy, just because Luke's not the guy for you doesn't mean that Trey is."

"Sam, I know you don't like Trey, but he's different than you think. He loves me. I know he has some rough edges that need smoothing, but please be happy for me. I'm happy for you and Charley."

She was. That was true, but she wasn't worried that Charley was after my money.

"You heard about Burt Lundy?" Both of us needed me to change the subject.

"Yes, but I can't get my head around it. He was such a rough guy that in some ways it makes more sense that someone would want to kill him. It's not the kind of stretch that it was with Elli and my aunt. It's still beyond awful, though."

"I guess it's a reminder that we should be happy when we can be. You know I love you and want the best for you, Lacy. You're a great person and friend."

"Me, too, you. I've got to go. He's going to bring some things over this evening."

She sounded happy. I was going to hang onto that.

"Oh, and here's some more news. They have someone they're talking to about Burt's murder. It's that Bob Smith. Do you know him? He's a kind of hard luck guy who's a mechanic at Moe's Garage. I guess Burt and he met when they were in jail together. That's how Bob ended up living here. Exciting, huh? Wouldn't it be nice if they actually had the killer? Maybe it *was* plain and simple robbery with Aunt Mabel."

"Why do they think it was this Bob?"

"Someone called, anonymously. Then Trey started to connect the dots. This Smith guy's fingerprints were at Burt's and they think at Elli's too."

"That's pretty sloppy work, isn't it? I mean suddenly someone who has eluded the police through two murders is leaving his fingerprints everywhere?"

"I guess. I just want the whole thing over. Besides, Trey says that Smith is a real no-goodnik. He rented one of Aunt Mabel's apartments, and once they got into a very loud argument over the rent."

"Did you hear the argument?"

"No, but I guess Aunt Mabel was worried enough about Smith that she called the police. Trey took the call."

Like Lacy, I wanted it all to be over. It would be so great to have everything back to normal.

I hung up, grabbed Messy's leash, and took a run. I wanted to celebrate the possible solving of the murders, my mother's truce with Charley, and Charley.

Messy raced so fast and joyfully that I felt immediate and crushing guilt for neglecting her runs. She's a real athlete and loves to show it. We raced around one block and then another. It was cold, but no snow yet. I could feel my breath in my ears.

I slowed a bit when a car seemed to be following us, but only for a minute because I remembered that Bob Smith was in jail and the town would soon be back to normal.

The car came up over the curb and headed straight for Messy and me. It was a great big old black car. I'm no expert on cars and paid little attention to the vehicle because I was whipping Messy around on her leash and heading us both in the opposite direction of the auto, which was too-rapidly approaching.

Our going in the opposite direction seemed to thwart the driver's intent. The car tore off in one direction, and I ran Messy in the other, right to the police station. It was closed. I forgot that this was the day Trey was moving into Lacy's.

I ran past the police station to the paper. "Somebody tried to run over us."

Scoop was sifting through the mail. "Sit down," he said. This time he got *me* coffee.

"Water, instead, please." I said.

I took Messy off her leash so she could get her fill of sniffs.

"Did you get a look at the car?" He handed me a glass of water.

"Big, black, old. I couldn't see the person. And I didn't get the feeling that he was trying very hard. Don't get me wrong. I'm thrilled to be here."

"Thrilled to have you." Scoop smiled. "Maybe it was Chloe Hite, mad because you've been messing around with her boyfriend."

"He's not her boyfriend. She's married." *My defensive behavior was showing.*

"Not any more. I hear she left Clarke a few days ago. He's desperate to have her back, even offered to put everything in her name, but she wants out. You wouldn't happen to know why she wants out, would you?"

"Not Charley. He's done with her."

"Looks like it." He looked out the window, and my eyes followed his to see Charley drive by with Chloe. My stomach sank to my knees. I didn't remember ever feeling so sick.

I couldn't speak.

"I tried to tell you, doll. He doesn't have it in him to be faithful. I'm sure he has a great line. I have a pretty good one or two myself, but that doesn't mean I can be trusted, and it certainly doesn't mean he can."

"Do you mind if we get to work." Get to work. That was a joke. I couldn't concentrate and felt like I was going to throw up every time I mentally replayed the image of Charley and Chloe. What I wanted to do was go over to his business and tell him to go to hell. I didn't, though, for two reasons. The first was that I was afraid what I might find there, and the second was that there might be an explanation a whole lot more satisfying that the one I'd conjured up. I'd love to prove Scoop wrong, but had little hope that I'd be able to.

I couldn't concentrate and Scoop raised no objection when I told him I was going to take Messy home and do some things around the house. I'd wait and see if Charley came to dinner, and if he did, I would serve *la spécialité de la maison*: Charley roasted to a crisp. Pardon my French!

My mother called to take me to dinner, but I told her I was already having dinner with Charley. She nervously chatted about several inconsequential subjects. She ended with, "Be careful." Obviously, Scoop had told her about the drive-by.

It wasn't going to be a big deal meal. I decided against pizza and stopped at The Ample Spoon to pick up Annette's burgundy pot roast, twice baked potatoes, garlic green beans, spinach salad, and cranberry apple pie. I'd make sure the condemned man had a hearty meal.

"Smells good." I can't tell you how good Charley looked, very casually but alluringly dressed in khaki slacks and a wine-colored sweater.

"Hope you didn't go to much trouble." He started to put his arms around me, but I moved away to put the pot roast on the table.

"Not much trouble at all." I'd be cool, casual, controlled. I'd planned it all day.

I lit the gas fireplace in the dining room. We'd eat before a roaring fire, before I roared.

The food was delicious and our eating was punctuated by one or two sentences once in a while.

"Something wrong?" He looked like he could not imagine anything being wrong.

This is where my plan went awry. Instead of finishing the meal first, I attacked.

"I think there *is* something wrong, Charley. I'm having such trouble reconciling what you have said to me with what I saw only a few hours ago."

"What I said about what?" Again, he seemed adrift as to what set me off.

"Don't you remember our conversation? Don't you remember telling me that you wanted to see if we had something together*?" What if he said he didn't remember? What if I'd dreamed the whole thing?*

"I meant what I said, Sam. Is that it? Are you afraid I didn't mean it?"

"How could I not be afraid when I watched you drive by with your old flame?"

For a minute he looked totally confused, so I almost thought I'd misinterpreted the whole situation. But then I realized that Charley had perfected his look of perplexed innocence when caught by one of his dates with another one of his dates.

"Chloe? You're still wound up about Chloe?" He'd gone pretty fast from confused to pissed off.

"Charley, I'm standing there telling my father that you're better than he thinks, and you drive by and prove he's right and that I'm a dope."

"And I can see why your dad feels that way. You, on the other hand, are another story. I've been honest with you about how I feel, and you still doubt me." I couldn't tell if he was angry or hurt. I started to feel that maybe I'd dug in a little too deeply.

"Chloe," he said, "has never been a serious consideration for me, a fact I've told her many times, but she keeps pushing. And over the years, sometimes she pushed just hard enough, when I was just weak enough, to get my attention. It never lasted long, and I made no promises. Today when I went home to shower, change, and go to work, I found her parked in front of my house. She was there a couple of days ago, too, to tell me she'd left her husband for me. I told her if she left him, it couldn't be for me because I was interested in someone else. She knows it's you. Today she got a little hysterical, shouting and saying she was going to hurt herself. I took her to the hospital in Grand Rapids. She's been there before. It's private, and no one needs to know. Chloe has bigger problems than her infatuation with me. I'm hoping this time she'll work on it. Clarke loves her and is there with her. We'll see."

"Charley, can you blame me for believing my own two eyes? It's not like she hasn't been part of your life."

"Let me ask you this: did you ever put your friend Yates through this kind of inquisition? Were there times you didn't trust him?"

"No." I was surprised he knew Yates' name.

"What it is about me that makes me less worthy than he is?"

"Nothing. It's just that Yates was . . . "

"Someone you could trust." He was red from his neck to his forehead. "You might have given up on him too quickly. It sounds like you and he are more suited. If you don't mind, I think I've had enough."

He left. I gulped and sobbed and between sobs stuffed everything I could get my hands on from cranberry apple pie to red wine into my mouth. By the time I was through, I couldn't remember Charley, and I couldn't have told anyone my name. I was totally plastered. So I did the only thing left to do, I passed out on the sofa, all the lights on, and the food still warm on the stove. Luckily, I'd already turned everything off, except my love for Charley and a drowning panic that Bob Smith had nothing to do with the murders.

Chapter Nine

I woke up the next morning with a Big Ten percussion section hopping around in my head and someone pounding on my door. My house reeked of overcooked everything. Messy's look was one of sheer disgust. Whoever was at the door was losing patience— loudly.

And there he was, just like I'd dreamed.

"You're not getting off this easily. God, you look awful." Charley was back, and he looked great.

"I thought you'd left forever." I knew I should be angry with him, but I was too hung over to remember why.

"You have a boyfriend with a short fuse. And you have a very sticky-looking but beautiful face." He wet a kitchen towel and gently cleaned wiped my face. "I'm working on my temper, but you have a way of pushing my buttons like no one else. Baby, you push everything like no one else." He held me to him. It helped my head, a little.

"Why are you back?" My sentences were still short and as fractured as my thoughts.

"The alternative is giving up on us. Not going to do that. And I have some news that you might be interested in."

"Kiss me," I said. "If you kiss me I'll know you love me."

He stepped back. "You're a pretty big mess, you know. You have something pretty awful wadded up in your hair. I'm going with pie, but if it's anything else, don't tell me."

"Kiss me."

He did, and he kissed me as if I'd just showered and had sprayed myself with Fendi. I loved him for that.

"Now, have I done enough penance?" He tugged at the pie tangled in my hair. "Believe me, you've looked better." He laughed as he pushed me toward the sofa in the living room. "Now let me tell you what I came to tell you."

"Tell!" I sat next to him and leaned my aching head on his shoulder.

"I don't think Bob Smith is the person who killed Elli, Mabel, and Burt. I have a guy who works for me named Wes Falls. He's a friend of Bob's and knows Burt. He says it's a setup. In fact, Wes says he knows for sure that Bob stayed with a woman the night of Burt's murder, but both Smith and his lady friend go to a very strict Pentecostal church that would condemn them for sleeping together before marriage. He couldn't tell the police where he really was so he gave them a pretty shaky alibi. Wes has had a long talk with Bob's girlfriend, and she's going to talk to Trey this morning."

"You are so smart." I kissed his neck.

"I think you may still be drunk, Miss Hayes. Exactly how much did you drink?" He walked over to the empty bottle of wine and two beers. "You're lucky you're alive."

"You're not mad at me for what I said last night?" I sounded far away.

"I'm furious, but I think I'm in love with you so I'll have to overlook your bad points."

"Love with me?" Because I couldn't absorb what he'd just said, I changed the subject, kind of, "How about if you help me wash? I might fall in the tub and hurt myself, you know."

"Anything for my lady."

****

Because Charley really knows his way around a shower, we didn't make it in time for breakfast at Mabel's, but we got there in time for lunch.

"You two look happy," Lacy gave us a knowing look, "and you look a little tired." She eyed me quizzically.

"She's had quite a night," Charley said, "and quite a morning."

"Quite a morning." I was still groggy, but I did manage to catch Annette Stancati staring at me from a corner table. Even in my wobbly state, I could see it was a scary stare. It made me feel pretty darn cool.

"Why don't you join us, Lacy—my treat?" Charley, oblivious to Annette's adoring glances, rose to pull out a chair.

"I would love to, but Trey's coming by later so we can spend some time together. We'll eat then. Do you want the regular, Sam?"

I nodded, and Charley ordered a Reuben on whole wheat and a cola. "Oh, and give us two of those double chocolate brownies," he added. "If you don't feel up to eating brownies," he looked very sweetly at me, "you can take yours home, little girl."

"So how are you, Charley?" Annette shot to our table as soon as Lacy left. It was as if I didn't exist. "I've been thinking of you." She was practically salivating.

"That's nice. The antipasto you brought over was much appreciated." Charley looked uncomfortable.

"That's what you said in your note," she gushed, still not seeing me. "It was a sweet note."

"I can't lie," he said, "my secretary wrote it."

"She has beautiful handwriting." Instead of leaving, Annette stood next to the table as if she had all the time in the world.

"Charley and I were talking about Burt Lundy's murder." I blasted right into the conversation.

"Oh, they have his killer," she quickly returned to Charley. "Anytime you want my antipasto, let me know."

"Maybe Sam and I could take you and your husband to dinner one night, as a thank you for being so kind." Charley stood to give her a signal that he was getting ready to leave and she should, too.

"I'd like that." But she slumped out of the restaurant.

"She has a crush on you," I whispered as I stood to leave.

"I have a crush on you, nasty disposition and all." He put his mighty arm around me and gave me a hug, right there in front of everyone.

"Just remember you said that," I said before I gave him a kiss right in front of everyone.

"Hey, no matter how much I wish I could be with you for the rest of the day, I have several things to accomplish. Should I walk you to the paper or drive you home?"

"It's Sunday, but I should go into the paper for a while. Walk me to work. I want to see what my father is up to, and I also want to make sure that Bob Smith is no longer Suspect Number One."

Charley dropped me off at The Corner News. I didn't blame him. Scoop was never easy on him.

"So you're still stuck on stupid." Scoop wasted no time rattling my cage.

"Charley is far from stupid, and you're far from the one who should talk. Let's table my love life and talk about Bob Smith."

"He didn't murder anyone or anything except his chances of being deacon at his church. He's free and that leaves us on square one."

"This whole thing can't be an accident."

"Nope. For sure, Burt was murdered." Scoop rooted around his desk trying to find a pen that worked.

"That's not what I mean. It can't be an accident that it's been weeks of searching and no one has a clear idea of who killed three people. Someone is impeding the investigation."

"But who? True, we're hampered by a cop without a brain, but I've talked to the state police and county sheriff. They, too, are befuddled. Love that word 'befuddled'."

"I'm going to Tweet something," I said.

"Head for the bathroom. This is a very small space."

"Funny. I'm going to put something on Twitter. I have hundreds of followers from that cupcake competition we ran over the Fourth of July. I'm going to see if we can draw out the murderer or someone who knows something about the murders."

"Don't use your name. I'm thinking that we have to do something," he rubbed his surprisingly clean-shaven face, "but I'm not sure this is what we should do."

"It's worth a try."

I pulled out my iPad and registered a new account on Twitter. My usual "handle" is Snoop@. This time I registered under my Hotmail address, which pretty much goes unused. My user name was now Cornered@.

But what to write? I sat at my desk feeling guilty that I had yet to assemble next week's *Snooping*. Still, I don't do well in limbo and needed more answers than anyone had come up with. The best idea I could come up with was, *Cotter's Corner is no place for murder, and we'll prove it soon. Beware.* Truthfully, I had little hope I'd draw out the bludgeoner, but knew I'd feel better trying.

I next eliminated a great deal of the work piled on my desk. When he deposited me in front of The

Corner News, Charley had told me he'd be with the attorneys for dinner that night. My mother was going to be sewing with Hilda and Aggie so I had the time to do what I wanted. By the time I left the paper, it was dark and Scoop had left hours before, so I locked up the paper and went home.

I regretted getting home so late because the house was pitch black when I walked inside. I'd left no light on for Messy. Oddly, she wasn't there to greet me or remind me how little she likes being left in the dark. "Messy?" No dog came bounding.

"Messy, girl?" Her not being there struck fear in me.

I felt cold air. Really cold. I turned on a light and made my way to the kitchen where a door—wide open—blasted cold air. Had I left it that way? Was Messy in the backyard? "Messy?" Again, no furry body raced toward me. Something was horribly wrong. I tore through the downstairs. Nothing. I ran upstairs. The hallway and guest bedroom were clear. Next was my room. Dread coursed through me.

I knew immediately she was in terrible trouble. There she was lying lifeless on my bed. "Oh, Messy!" I hugged her to me. Thank God she lifted her head, but barely.

And when she began to let her head drop back down, I saw the blood. I grabbed my phone from the nightstand and dialed as I looked at the note lying next to the blood. It read, "Cornered @ Dead." That was all it said, but my spinning head knew that Messy had been shot because of me. Someone *had* been drawn out by my Tweet and that someone had hurt my wonderful girl. I could barely get a breath, but when I did, I cried into the phone.

"Please come quick. I need your car to help me get Messy to the vet's. She's bleeding all over. I think she's been shot!"

Without questioning putting a bloody dog in her new luxury auto, my mother was at my house within minutes. "Oh, look at that poor darling." She helped me lift Messy and carry her almost lifeless body down the stairs and into her car. Then she drove like a bat out of hell to get us to the twenty-four hour emergency vet ten minutes away.

"Will she live?" I asked over and over as the vet examined her.

"She's lost a considerable among of blood, and the bullet is lodged pretty close to her heart. It's going to be tricky." Dr. Sherrod was as kind as she could be, but what she said still nearly paralyzed me. I'd thought of a lot of awful things lately, but losing my Messy had never been one of them. What would I do without her?

They took her into surgery, and my mother and I waited. And waited and waited.

When I thought I couldn't bear the tension one more minute, Charley burst through the door. "Sam?" And right there in front of my mother, he grabbed me and kissed me maybe a thousand times. "Oh, Sam, I dropped some Cotter Foundation papers off at your mother's and Mrs. Patterson told me she'd raced to your house because of a shooting. No one was there and I called the hospitals. I've driven all over looking for your mother's car."

"Oh, Charley, it's Messy, not me." I stayed wrapped in his arms. "I think Messy might die."

"Nonsense!" my mother said as if she knew. "Messy will be just fine. She's a strong girl. It's nice of you to come, though, Charley."

Then the three of us sat and waited and waited some more. Several other patients entered the office while the vet operated on my dog. One was a man with a retriever who had a tennis ball lodged in his mouth. Another was a woman who had run out of her dog's tranquilizers. And the last was a man whose dog had been hit by a car and who wanted its body cremated. His heartbreak gave me a sense of what I could be in store for. I tried to stop crying, but couldn't. My mother and Charley stayed with me, he with his arm firmly around me, and she holding my hand. A little before midnight, the veterinarian returned. She was covered in blood, my dog's blood.

"It's been a long night," she said, "and we still have a way to go with your dog, but I think she just might make it."

I couldn't stop crying. Finally between sobs, I asked, "Can I stay here, with her?"

"She's going to have to be kept pretty drugged, and we'll watch her through the night. We don't really have accommodations for visitors, that aren't furry," she smiled.

"I'll just sleep sitting up here. Please, I've pretty much ignored her lately so I want to be here for her now."

"Sure," she said.

"I'll follow your mother to make sure she gets home safely and then I'll be back." Charley kissed me.

"No, there's something else you can do," I whispered as my mother talked to the vet about the bill, which she insisted on paying. "Someone was in my house. The window on the back door is smashed in and there's a short note on the bed that the person who did this to Messy left. Would it be asking too much to have you call the county police and get them over to

investigate. Maybe there are fingerprints on the note."
I knew the county police couldn't say no to Charley.

"Done." He waited for my mother to pay Messy's bill, which I couldn't' keep her from doing. Then Charley and she left.

I leaned back against the concrete wall and slept fitfully.

Sunlight was streaming in through the windows, and people were in the office when I woke up. Dr. Sherrod was standing in front of me.

"It's as I thought. That's a very strong girl you have there. In fact, she'll be ready to go home this afternoon if I can get you to promise you'll keep her lying down and calm. I don't think that will be any problem, though; she's exhausted from all that she's been through. But I get the idea that your Messy loves both you and her home and will recuperate faster there than here."

"Thank you." I actually hugged Dr. Sherrod. My knees and arms ached with relief. "Oh," I said to the vet before she returned to Messy, "could I borrow your phone? I need to call for a ride."

"Your ride's here." Scoop appeared out of nowhere. "Charley had to be in New York and wanted to make sure you get home safely. I'm taking you to your mother's since there are workmen at your house."

"Workmen?"

"You know your mother. First thing this morning she had men there fixing your door and putting in a state-of-the art alarm system. She insisted I take you to her house until they're through."

"But Messy?"

"I've already arranged for the doctor to let us know when she's ready to be picked up later today. Your mother or I will do it."

"I think this is the first time that you and she have ever worked together on anything."

He laughed, "Wonders never cease, right?"

"Right."

I talked Scoop into stopping at the paper so I could pick up some things to work on. What we'd intended to be a quick stop turned into half an hour due to phone calls and an ad I forgot had to be done the day before.

The coffee was cold and tasted awful, but would, I hoped, keep me awake until I could jump into my mother's shower.

"So you got a response for that thing you sent?"

"Sent?"

"That Twit thing."

"Oh, the Tweet. Yes, that was brilliant. It got my dog shot."

"No, your smart idea may have drawn out someone mean enough to kill three people and shoot a helpless dog."

"Do you have any idea who would do this?"

"I thought the Smith guy was a good possibility. He knew Burt and has a shady past. He also has probably been down on his luck and might have tangled with Mabel. Elli might have been collateral damage. But Smith isn't the guy, or so we're told. What we do know is that it has to be someone from around here, someone who's watching the town and you."

Luke Barrett walked into the paper so Scoop and I clammed up.

"I need to change my ad. I'm selling the agency and want people to know the new owners. Here's some information about them." Luke looked a little deflated.

"I'm sorry you're selling. Does that mean you're leaving?"

"I'm taking over an uncle's agency in Palm Beach. At first we thought we'd hold onto this, but it would mean too much back and forth. The Palm Beach agency is highly profitable so this is the one to let go."

"I'm really sorry to see you go."

I was. I wished Lacy could have liked him. Maybe that would have encouraged him to make a go of the agency. He was sure a lot better than the guy she did like.

Charley phoned soon after Luke left so I filled him in on Messy, though he already knew because he'd called the vet's just after Scoop and I left. I also mentioned that Luke had sold his agency.

"I think I heard someone talking about it," Charley said. "I guess he needs to be in Florida. He's kind of doing the opposite of me. I'm selling the Florida places and consolidating the businesses so I can be in Cotter's Corner. Is it all right if I hang around more?"

"I guess." Hurray!

Scoop was pointing to his wristwatch and signaling he wanted to leave.

"I'm going to my mother's for a shower and maybe a nap before we pick up Messy. How about I call you later?"

"No need. I'm going to wind up things here and should be back in town right after supper. I just talked with the foreman who's overseeing the work at your house. He says that they won't be done until tomorrow morning. Since there's no way your mother will let you stay in that house without an alarm system, how about if I pick you up at her house when I get back? You can stay with me. Messy's invited, too."

"Charley, my mother lives right next door. I don't think staying overnight with you is going to win her over."

"Au contraire, my dear. It's your mother's idea. She has a dinner date with that lawyer from Grand Rapids she's been seeing. She volunteered to break it, but I convinced her that you'll be even safer at my house with me watching over you. Besides, she's feeling a little bit better about me since I put her on The Cotter Foundation Board."

"Should I be worried? That's pretty manipulative of you."

"Be afraid. Be very afraid."

I couldn't lie. The idea of going back to my house alone gave me the heebie jeebies. And the idea of spending time in Charley's house had a far pleasanter effect on me.

****

"You've done some work here." I looked around Charley's living room with its elegant crown moldings and museum-quality antiques.

"When I decided to be a grownup, I hired a designer. I told her to make it casually and warmly elegant. What do you think?"

"I think she did what you asked." All inviting greens and golds with ivory trim, the house flowed smoothly from one large, luxurious room to the other. "I love this fountain." I had forgotten that right in the middle of his foyer, Charley had a working marble fountain.

"I thought about getting rid of it," he said, "but this was the house we lived in while my mother was alive and the fountain was her idea. When push came to shove, I couldn't give it up. And dad still couldn't bring himself to sell it, even when he built the monstrosity next door."

"Which is now my mother's monstrosity," I reminded him.

"True, but I gave her a great deal, sort of a friends and family discount. I'm buying her good opinion. Now to more important business." He kissed me long, hard, and deep.

Much as I would like to have continued the activity we'd just begun, there was something more important. "We'd better get Messy upstairs." My dog had been able to walk from the vet's office to the car, but we'd lifted her up and in. Now she was sitting with a dazed expression in his foyer. Charley carried her up the circular staircase.

Charley's bedroom is straight out of *Architectural Digest*. I didn't allow my mind to wander to the X-rated activities he might have engaged in there. Instead, I watched the loving way he placed Messy on his lush comforter without a second thought. "That should make you feel better," he petted her.

His bedroom is a suite with floor to ceiling bay windows and a bathroom bigger than my living room. It was out of one of those large windows that I spied a very familiar junk heap pulling into my mother's winding driveway.

"Does Scoop visit often?" I asked Charley, who continued to shower Messy with attention.

"I guess." Charley fed Messy another doggie treat. "Does it bother you? I mean, the thought of your parents getting cozy?"

"Sure. They have a history of fireworks and mini-explosions. No truce between them has lasted longer than a few weeks."

"It's *their* history, though. Maybe we should leave it to them and concentrate on making our own history."

"It's my history, too, Charley. He made my mother's life pretty miserable, and thus mine was not so much fun either."

"Seems like she's forgiven him." He was giving me those kisses behind my ears and on my neck that drive me wild.

"Oh, poor Scoop. There he goes backing out of the driveway. I hope my mother and that fellow in Grand Rapids make a great couple." I relaxed and gave myself over to Charley's hungry demands.

Later that night, Charley and I sat in front of the fire, each of us in one of his plush robes. Only then did I let the awful part of my world sneak back in.

"I know I have to go home, but the thought of someone in there to do me and Messy harm holds me back."

"Great. We'll just move you in here," he kissed me.

"Lovely but not helpful. Now be serious for a minute."

"Sure thing, Ms. Hayes."

"I need a pep talk. You need to tell me that everything is going to be okay—that all of this creepy stuff will disappear as fast as it came."

"Oh, darlin,' I wish I could." No fooling around this time, just his searing, beautiful eyes connecting the two of us. "There's something in this town that is pure evil."

I pulled the robe up around my neck. Even the fire couldn't warm me after Charley spoke. "I want to be safe," I said. There was my motivating factor most of my life: safety. The safe college, the safe boyfriend, the safe town. All that was now a house of cards.

"As long as I have breath in my body," he crushed me to him. "I'll see that you're safe."

"I wish you could." I wrapped my arms around him and would have stayed there forever if his doorbell hadn't rung.

"There you are!" Aggie pushed through the door with Hilda, wide as she was tall, following in Aggie's wake. "You might tell someone what's going on." Her eyes breathed fire.

"I tried," Charley said, "Sam's mother told me to call, and I did just before I took off for New York this morning. Then I forgot."

Aggie's expression said Charley was still not a favorite and this oversight didn't help plead his case.

"We looked everywhere for you, even called Trey," Hilda said. "We wanted to make sure you wasn't the next victim. Your mother wasn't home and we couldn't find her either." Hilda, no spring chicken, was breathless. "But you did good about Bob Smith," she said. "You know he's Bub's nephew, right? Bub, me, and Aggie want to take you to the Moose Hall for wild game night in a couple of weeks, our treat. Bob's not a bad guy, and we're grateful for all you did."

"That's so sweet." I returned Hilda's hug, hoping she didn't know I'd avoided eating wild game most of my life. "I didn't really do anything. I think it was his girlfriend who helped." I sat there naked beneath the robe and amazed that our unexpected guests seemed oblivious to the fact. "I'm glad though. I mean I'm glad he's free."

"I'm sure it was you. His girlfriend let Bob help himself to a lot of things, but I don't think she was any help in this." Hilda rolled her lid-heavy eyes.

"Now he's a bit of a sinner," Aggie said. "He knows better than to be shacking up with anyone. Our church says it's a sin, but they was both baptized in the church, and they're coming Sunday to ask for forgiveness. And if you ask me, it was more her fault that his. It's a man's place to ask but a woman's place to say no, you know."

"Apologize to who?" I couldn't imagine poor Bob and his long-in-the tooth honey having to apologize to anyone for their relationship.

"The congregation, of course. Bob and her will stand before us all, confess what they did and then promise it won't happen again." Hilda stood ramrod as straight as her osteoporosis would allow when she pronounced the church's position.

"And it won't happen again," Hilda chimed in, "because they're getting married right after their confession. We're not taking any chances. You only get one chance not to burn in hell."

Not a peep from Charley who, I was sure, was having a hard time not bursting into gales of laughter. And I wasn't sure how Aggie and Hilda's newfound righteousness reconciled with their pasts, but that was their business.

"Where's your mom? We were going to invite her to sew with us tomorrow." Thankfully, Aggie changed the subject.

"I think she's on a date."

"With your father?" Hilda's eyes narrowed.

"No. She's seeing someone from Grand Rapids."

"That's more like it," Aggie said. "That old coot— sorry, Sam, I know he's your father—gave her grief, a lot of it, a while ago and he doesn't need to do it again."

"I feel the same way," I patted her arm, "but it's her life."

"Well," Aggie closed the conversation, "me and Hilda are going back to my place to sew. I know you haven't been sewing squares lately, so get back to it, okay?"

"You know Messy was shot, right?" I blurted it out as it popped into my mind. *Had anyone told Aggie?*

Aggie looked like she was going to faint. She obviously hadn't been told. As calmly as possible, I related the previous night's scare.

"Damn! It wasn't on the scanner, and I guess we aren't the friends I thought we were or you would care about telling an old lady what's going on." She fired a blast of fury at me, grabbed Hilda by the arm, wheeled her around, and pushed her out the door.

"You got some 'splainin' to do with Aggie, Lucy." Charley obviously thought the whole thing was much funnier than I did.

"You don't know Aggie. I'm going to have to do something really nice to win her back."

"She adores you. Give her a few days."

"I'm not one to criticize, but it might have helped if someone had thought to tell her."

"So now it's my fault." Charley played hurt and angry. It worked. Make up sex really is the best.

Chapter Ten

Charley left for Chicago early the next morning, but not before he helped me get a vastly improved Messy out to do *her business*, as Messy and I have come to refer to it. Then he made up a bed for her in the corner of the living room on one of the most expensive sofa cushions I'd ever seen. He was a good guy. Messy was already in love with him, and I was pretty much there myself.

I left Messy in the very capable hands of Charley's housekeeper and went next door to have coffee with my mother. She was so apologetic for not being around the previous evening that she insisted I come over so she could make it up to me.

Somewhere, and not in Cotter's Corner, my mother picked up unbelievably delicious sticky buns. We had those with her housekeeper Mrs. Patterson's homemade hazelnut lattés. "So good," was all I could say with my mouth full of the gooey lusciousness.

"Are you going to tell me about last night?" she coaxed.

"No, but you can fill me in on your date."

"Not a date really, more of a dud. John's a nice guy, but he has quite an ego. I'm never going to put up with a narcissist again."

"There!" I jumped up. "You admit that Leland is egomaniacal! Thank God!"

"Be loyal, Sam," she shook her finger at me. "He was very good to both of us."

"And then he wasn't," I reminded her.

"Look around, Sam. He could have left me far less well off."

"Okay. It's a great house. It's a big, beautiful, jaw-dropping house, but if I had to sleep with Leland, I would . . . ."

"Stop!" she interrupted my rudeness. "You are perilously close to getting a spanking."

"You're right. I'll keep quiet on the Leland subject. Anyway, he's history."

"I wish."

"He's not history?" I felt that creepy, crawly feeling you get in those slasher movies when you see the killer before the next victim does.

"He's been calling a lot lately, but only because little Thurgood seems to be a little handful. And the judge seems to want Leland's name and his influence, but she's not so sure she wants him around full time. She's keeping her own place and staying with him on weekends."

"You mean he's complaining about a child he only has around a couple of days a week?" *What chance did I ever have?*

"You make him sound unreasonable. I know he's rigid, but I also know that he's making an attempt to make the new marriage work."

"Ok, I know I'm hovering in 'unfriending' territory, but I'm going to say it anyway. When he was married to you, he was cheating with her. Now he's married to her and calling you for comfort. Are we seeing a pattern here?"

"Yes, I know what he's up to. And I know that I could never go back to him. But we were together for a long time. I owe him some understanding."

"But only understanding. Don't offer him conjugal comfort, and for god's sake, don't offer to have him here."

She paused. "Not even if he stays at a hotel?"

"Not even."

She sighed.

"Oh, and Aggie and Hilda came looking for you and seemed relieved that you weren't out on a date with Scoop. Am I missing something here? Do I need to get an interventionist to shake you back to sanity?"

"He's different."

"Different than what? An orangutan? A civilized human being? What?"

"He's different than he used to be. And that's all I'm going to say, except that I'm never getting married again. I've done that twice and have no belief that the third time's a charm. But you are not one to talk."

"What do you mean?" I was well aware of why she was diverting the issue.

"Charley. You have given me a dozen promises that you will have nothing to do with him, and then last night you . . . ."

"Out of bounds!" I stopped her. "And I'll use your excuse: he's different."

"He is."

"You agree? This is Charley we're talking about. Charley Cotter, your sworn enemy."

"But he is different from the way he was, or the way I thought he was. I see it, and it's not merely because he's put me on his foundation's board. And don't get me wrong, I still have many, many, many reservations about him, but I see the way he looks at you and the way he treats you. He was wonderful last night."

"He was." My mind began to wander dreamily to the next time I would see Charley.

"The men in my life always leave me." It was as personal as my mother ever got. "First my father, though he couldn't help being killed in that accident.

And then Aunt Cathy's husband was so emotionally disconnected, and we all know what a charmer your father was. By the time I got to Leland, I never expected someone to be tender and caring. I only wanted him to stay and keep me safe. That didn't happen either, did it?"

"So why are you again wading into the deep end with Scoop?"

"He's not drinking. Alcohol was always his catalyst for disaster. He knew it even back then but was powerless to control it. He was also overwhelmed trying to keep both the paper financially afloat and a wife and child happy. He wasn't built to be responsible for others. He escaped to the bottle."

"You make it sound all right that he found an escape hatch and left you to handle everything."

"Yes he did. And in these past few weeks, he's apologized a thousand times over."

"But it won't last."

"Let's give him some credit. He's had a couple of health scares lately, and I think he knows that drinking will kill him."

"Health scares?" I'd never considered a time when my aggravating father wouldn't be around.

"His blood pressure is higher than it should be and so is his cholesterol. The doctor gave him a real talking to. That coincided with my coming here. Sam, I've never doubted your father loved me. I've always doubted his constancy. We'll see. And, since we're talking so frankly, let's not give me too much of a break. I'm a snob and a witch when I want to be. I don't see that totally changing either, do you?" She laughed as she handed me another sticky bun which meant I would skip lunch and probably dinner to make up for calories I was jamming into my mouth.

"Now that we have Thanksgiving over," my mother changed subjects as badly as she changed lanes, "let's talk about Christmas."

"Bodies are all over this town and you want to talk about Christmas." I couldn't help laughing.

"We have to think of something happy and you know how much I love to shop. This year I have a great idea for presents for Aggie and Hilda."

"And the presents are?"

"New sewing machines, wonderful new sewing machines. I'm going to get myself one, and I'm buying each of them one."

"They'll never accept them. Aggie won't let me do anything big for her."

"I have my ways," my mother said. "Basically I'm going to tell them that this Christmas I want to thank them for giving me a life. That part is totally true. I've also ordered engraved Bibles with their names on them. God and I have a rather impersonal relationship, but I admire their faith."

"I have to say you are a very good person." Normally I would have added "when you want to be" but that kind of anger at my mother seemed remarkably absent lately.

"I want to go to Grand Rapids tomorrow for the sewing machines. Since you're at Charley's until at least the afternoon—oh so the workers tell me—his housekeeper can keep an eye on Messy. Come on. I'll even buy you a sewing machine. We need you to move faster on making those quilt squares or whatever Aggie calls them. The sewing machine store I have in mind advertises a huge variety of quilt fabrics."

"I like Aunt Cathy's machine," I said. "I don't need a big fancy one."

"No one's going to take Cathy's machine away from you, but you'll love the new quilters' machines.

You can pick out whatever one you think will work for you."

"But what happens when you get tired of it?"

"I don't think I'll tire of a new machine. I've missed the creative process involved in sewing."

"I mean what happens when you get tired of this new persona, this woman who is a back to basics woman? Mother, no offense, but I can't see you giving up Neiman Marcus forever."

"Neither can I, dear, but it doesn't have to be the either or world I boxed myself into these past couple of decades. And I do love my new life. I can't imagine ever wanting to go back to ladies' lunches and yearly cosmetic surgery procedures."

"Then, sure. I'll go. But I'm buying dinner. I know a great place." I didn't respond to the other part of our discussion. I hoped my mother saw herself accurately and that it all didn't go away one day.

I was asleep when Charley got in bed that night.

"Shhh.," he said wrapping his arms around me. "It's all right. Go back to bed."

I slept safe and sound with Messy snoring at the foot of the bed.

"No." Charley was adamant the next morning when I told him I was going with my mother to Grand Rapids.

"No?" I couldn't believe he thought I needed his permission.

"No. Your mother is not driving. My driver Harrison will take you. I'll be in town all day so I have no need for him to pick me up at the airport. He's not busy enough to suit him so he'll appreciate the drive to Grand Rapids. And I'll feel better having you take the limo, given what's been going on. That way, he can drop you off at home and check the place out. I'll meet you there later."

"A limo, huh? What if some hot guy thinks I'm a movie star and wants me to take him home?" I teased.

"You tell him that there's a hot, hungry guy waiting at home for you." His kiss said he wasn't kidding.

Right before Harrison and I pulled up in front of my mother's house an hour later, I called Aggie to tell her my mother and I would be out of town for the day. I asked her to tell Hilda. "I will." Her tone was cool. I was still being punished. I'd pick up some material and new scissors for her and Hilda. I couldn't stand it when she gave me the cold shoulder. She was my rock, my craggy rock, but my much-loved one.

I wasn't worried about Messy. She would be fine. In fact, she'd become quite the lady of leisure. I wondered if she could do more than she pretended. Did she really need to be carried all over the house and up and down the stairs? And were those soulful eyes of hers really in pain or was that just her way of getting extra dog treats?

The ride to Grand Rapids was a whole other experience in a limousine with a trusty driver. I checked my iPad for emails, and my mother listened to an audiobook on her iPod. The limo housed assorted juices and sparkling water as well as dozens of expensive cheeses and crackers. Leland's lifestyle had been lavish, but Charley's took *over the top* way over the top. It wasn't hard to get used to. As I was responding to Rose's email, I realized I'd told her at least half a dozen times I would visit soon. Right then I promised myself that as soon as the murderer was caught and shackled, I would treat Rose to a trip to Cotter's Corner. She could use a break, and I wanted her to meet Charley. I'd told her bits and pieces about our relationship, but since she was in the thick of it when I was waffling between marrying Yates and breaking up with him, I knew she was worried that this new guy was one big mistake.

We hit Grand Rapids and my mother hit the stores like Sherman took Atlanta. She was a woman on a mission. Within an hour, she'd purchased four sewing machines. I insisted I didn't need one, and she insisted I did. Enough said. Since each machine probably cost more than the down payment on either Aggie's or Hilda's house, I still wasn't totally sure they'd accept them. But I loved this version of my mother that was eager to do something for someone else.

I picked up the best sewing scissors I could find for Aggie and got sewing baskets for her and Hilda for Christmas. I also got them gift certificates to the sewing machine store which had a wide array of fabric and patterns for quilts. Both Aggie and Hilda would go nuts over the store's quilting materials. As part of their Christmas present, I'd take them to the store in Grand Rapids and end at their favorite restaurant Applebee's.

I directed Harrison to one of my favorite restaurants as my mother read the sewing machine's instruction book. "I'm so glad it comes with this," her excitement was childlike. "So many companies are putting their manuals on the Internet, but what do people like Aggie and Hilda, who don't have computers, do? Hey, maybe I should get them computers?"

"Simmer down, Mommy Big Bucks," I laughed as we pulled up to the restaurant. "Baby steps with Aggie and Hilda. They're proud women who have survived on their own. They give to charity, but hate to take it."

"You're right. I'll be sly and pick my moments."

It wasn't exactly what I'd said, but there was no changing her completely. Baby steps with my mother, too.

Messy was great was the message I got from Charley. He'd gone home from work to check on her.

What a guy, I thought to myself. *Please don't let this all be a dream.*

"Sam, this is charming," my mother said it like she meant it as she studied the restaurant's interior after being seated. She'd urged Harrison to join us, but he said he was eating a big meal with his wife's family the next day so he was going to eat the salad and sandwich that he'd put in the limo's fridge.

"My mother would like your lobster salad," I said to the pleasant woman serving us, "and I'd like your Reuben."

"Change mine to a Reuben, too," my mother said, "I never get them, and I do like them. But make mine turkey. Oh, and please have a huge vanilla shake delivered to the limo parked just to the right in the front. And charge me for delivery." Mother turned to me and winked. "If all he has is a salad and sandwich, the shake can't hurt too much."

"Unless he's diabetic," I laughed.

"Hope not. I hadn't thought of that. Maybe I should send him something low cal."

"Mom, I'm kidding. Harrison doesn't look like he's turned down too many meals."

"Do you come here much? It's nice. Really nice." We were waiting for our order and my mother was fiddling with a broken nail.

"Lacy and I come here three or four times a year. We used to come more, but Trey doesn't like fancy restaurants. I think he just likes to eat free at Lacy's place."

"I have to meet this Trey. He sounds like a dope."

"Dope. Now that's a word you don't hear much but really quite perfect for him. Perfect."

We devoured our Reubens and were studying the dessert menu when someone in a far-off corner, a dark one, caught my eye. The girl looked a little familiar, but it took a minute to place her. The man she was with, however, was immediately recognizable. Trey Davis looking as snaky as ever, pored over the menu. The beautiful young girl with him was none other than Burt Lundy's daughter and Elli's drop-dead-gorgeous great-niece, Jenny Lundy.

I averted my head before Trey spotted me spotting him. Disgust replaced what had been the meal's pleasant effect. Lacy trusted this guy, and there he sat with an adorable little girl. Well, I studied Jenny for only a second, but saw that she was now far from a little girl—and that third button down definitely needed to be buttoned up!

"Isn't that girl the one who works for Lacy at Mabel's?"

"Shh!" I stopped my mother. "Look down. I don't want them to know we see them."

"Them?" My mother leaned in and whispered conspiratorially. "Do you know the man she's with?"

"You might say I do," I whispered back. "It's Trey Davis."

"Lacy's Trey?" My mother sat bolt upright. "The dog!"

"Mother, calm down. We need to get out of here. I don't want him to know we spotted him."

"Well," she lowered her tone again, "maybe they're just friends."

"Look at where his hand is," my eyes signaled to look below the table.

"Oh, my lord!" My mother was too loud, and for a second I was worried we were discovered, but that hand and Trey's libido seemed to have impeded his hearing.

"We need to leave." I put down the tip and started to rise, but out of the corner of my eye, I spotted movement. "Don't get up," I hissed. "Look at the bill as if we're trying to figure out the tip."

No need. I could see as Jenny and Trey left through the far door that they had eyes and hands only for each other.

"That was quite a display," my mother's prim and proper self returned.

"I'm just sick for Lacy," I said. "She thinks they're serious."

"Well, she might be, but he looked anything but the devoted beau. Are you going to tell her?"

"I don't know. If I do, it will break her heart. But if I don't, her life will be a mess. What do you think I should do?"

The look on my mother's face told me she realized I hadn't asked her for advice since we went bra shopping when I was way past the bra shopping era of my friends. Not to worry, though, in the long run, my breasts were just fine, thank you.

"You save the hard questions for me," she said as Harrison pulled the limo up to the front of the restaurant. "It's a problem. My best friend told me about Leland and his judge friend. I didn't speak to her for months, but I'm now in constant touch with her. She's the best—and perhaps the only—true friend I had in Chicago. All the others kept quiet, but talked about me behind my back."

"I think you've answered my question," I smiled.

"Thanks for the milkshake," Harrison said as he opened the limo's door for us. "Don't know when I've had better." I scooted over for my mother to get in. Then Harrison returned to the driver's seat. Turning the key, he pointed us toward home.

My mother slept during the hour-drive to Cotter's Corner. I, however, could think of nothing but the heartbreak sure to befall Lacy when I told her about

Trey and Jenny. I wanted to believe it was a harmless lunch, but there was no mistaking the intimate smiles and touches. I'd never seen Trey that familiar with Lacy. It was a mess, through and through. If I told Lacy, I would hand her already pain-filled life more pain and suffering. If I kept quiet, I ensured her a life with someone she couldn't trust when he was out of her sight.

Chapter Eleven

We got home just before the storms started. Scoop was waiting for us at my mother's and helped Harrison unload the sewing machines. Charley's security guard left his post to help too.

I left my mother with Scoop and let Harrison drive me home. I dreaded getting there and having the awful feeling that a stranger had not long before entered my house and nearly killed my dog.

But no need to worry. Charley was at my house waiting for me and seeing him removed all those fears of hating to be in the house. Messy was something else. I swear she missed the glitz and ease of life at Charley's. She barely wagged her tail.

"Do you think she's all right?" I asked.

"She's fine," Charley smiled. "Watch." He reached into his pants pocket and drew out a biscuit.

Messy was up and practically dancing. The force of her tail literally wiped magazines from my coffee table.

"You little faker," I patted her. "This is your life. Live with it."

"Thanks," I turned to Charley and wrapped my arms around him, "but I don't have a cookie for you."

"I'll take my treats in other ways. Woof! Woof!"

****

Christmas was three weeks away and we were no closer to finding the murderer. That was the first thought that hit me the next morning. The second was the excitement that rushed over me when I saw a tousled blonde head on my pillow. What a great way to wake up.

"For a second, I forgot you were here," I said as I snuggled against him.

"I'm not sure I like being forgettable. I'm going to have to do something to change all that. Is this all still hard for you to take in?"

"What all?" I asked as I let his arms encircle me.

"You know what I mean. Sometimes when we're together, I can't totally believe that I'm actually with Sam Hayes."

"And I'm with Charley Cotter." It took on a surreal feeling as soon as I said it.

"Who else?" he kissed my neck. "I'm going to go downstairs and make pancakes for my love."

My love. I was too thrown by it to address what Charley said. Instead, I changed the subject.

"Could we talk for just a minute?"

"I've been so good," he groaned. "It can't be about us."

"It's not. *Us* are perfect. It's about yesterday in Grand Rapids. I saw Jenny Lundy with Trey."

I then went on to give him the gory details. "So do I tell Lacy?" I asked. "It could kill our friendship."

"Why don't you let me tell her that I'm the one who saw them?" he volunteered.

"I can't. Lacy and I go way back, I'm either going to tell her the truth or tell her nothing."

"Let's get you some breakfast first," he pulled me from the silky sheets. "I may have another idea or two for giving you some fortification. I think that's the word."

Thunder and lightning danced around as Charley drove me to work. The drive, though short, gave me a couple of seconds to think of Scoop. He had changed. I feared the change would be short-lived and disappointing, but lately he'd been almost civil, almost enjoyable. I knew my mother's appearance in town had affected him positively, but I had little hope that the change would be permanent. They hadn't been good for each other in the past and wouldn't, I was sure, be any better for each other now.

"I'll be tied up with work here and there for the next few days, but I'll call," Charley pulled my coat around my neck as he kissed me goodbye. "Stay warm until I return."

I walked into the newspaper and thought to myself that I wasn't worried that Charley would be with anyone else. He'd managed to convince me that for him, there was no one else. That thought kept me plenty warm.

It was an unusual and violent thunderstorm for December, which usually means tornadoes or some other violent occurrence. I hoped this was the exception. To get over my "It was a dark and stormy night" jitters, I drafted my next *Snooping* column. I knew it would please my mother to have something about her sewing with Aggie and Hilda. I also put in something about Sally Hatfield winning the Bingo tournament at Holy Family Catholic Church, and at the last minute I scrounged up Lacy's mother's recipe for Cherry-Almond Cheesecake, perfect for the holidays. Lacy would appreciate the journalistic tribute to her late mother.

The thunder shaking the office and being alone shook me. Every once in a while, the lightning caused the lights to flash on and off. I grabbed a pile of papers off Scoop's desk to see if he'd left any unfinished work to keep me focused. Murders all around and thunder and lightning were enough to scare even the sturdiest person. All that was needed to make the scene perfectly horrid was Freddy Krueger jumping out at me.

As I corrected Scoop's typos and turned his dangling participles into coherent sentences, I tried to find a common denominator for the three murder victims. Was it possible that Charles Cotter, Sr., decided to take his life, or had some part of what had happened to Elli, Mabel, and Burt played into his desperate act? One question reverberated: *How*? *How could four such disparate human beings have been connected in any way?* One was an eighty-some-year-old woman, another was a prominent, hard-bitten businesswoman, the third was the town derelict, and the fourth was one of Michigan's and the country's most powerful men. Scoop and I had both tried every which way to draw a connection, but it didn't happen. Had Elli learned something that connected the dots? Had Mabel cornered someone who was meaner and tougher than she? Burt? He knew all kinds of dark and dangerous characters. Had loser Burt, known for his own share of skullduggery, fallen into a deadly trap without knowing it? But that still left Charley's dad, a mysterious figure in his own right and said to be plagued by depression and rumors.

And why had Bob Smith been thrown into the mix? He appeared to be the sacrificial lamb, but why had he been sacrificed and by whom?

The lights went totally out. I could hear my breath becoming staccato. Footsteps, coming too fast for me to stop them. Hands went on my shoulders and just before I screamed, I felt Charley's cheek against mine. "Here you are. I had a bad feeling when I left you off so I thought I'd make sure you weren't alone here."

And as he spoke, the lights returned.

I burrowed into his tweed coat. "I don't think I've ever been happier to see you."

"Then I'm doubly glad I came back." He kissed the top of my head. "This is one of the saddest times in my life, and thanks to you, I'm happy." He pulled away and studied me. "There are those wonderful eyes that eat into my soul. And, of course, those lips." He kissed me, and I was again sixteen gasping for air, and not because I'd nearly drowned.

"You make me believe everything will be fine." I whispered into his coat.

"Tonight, how about if I make you feel safe all night long? I've decided to put off anymore out-of-town trips until this town simmers down. By the way, at what were you staring so intently when I looked through the window?"

"I was thinking about the murders." No need to tell him about my questions regarding his father. "Have you come up with any genius idea of what's going on?"

"I've been busy trying to update the new director of The Foundation, but that's coming along nicely. Your boyfriend is a brilliant businessman, did you know that? Sorry to report I'm not as brilliant on the murder front."

"You could make it so much better if you'd just solve these darn things." I kissed him. I'm not usually the kisser, more like the kissee, but that mouth and that skin that warm to my touch were irresistible.

"Maybe I'll stop in more often. I like this side of you. Crazy about me, aren't you?"

"Crazy," I said and then I kissed and kissed and kissed him.

"How about if we slip over to my house?" His mouth was hot against my hair.

"I can't leave the paper and I have no idea where Scoop is. He said he was coming here, but I don't see him."

"He's doing this to ruin our chance at happiness, you realize that don't you? Well, since you're not having any of what I'm offering, I'm going to get to work. Oh, and I'm crazy about you, too."

"Is that a good thing?"

"That, my sweet, darling, sexy-as-hell Sam, is a very good thing." He kissed me so sensually that he literally nearly knocked me off my feet. "I just can't get enough of you. And on that note," he added, "I promise you that with the Cotter Corporation running smoothly and once The Foundation gets back to normal, I won't give you a moment's rest."

Charley gave me one last indescribably tender and perfect kiss. Somehow he manages to be strong yet tender, demanding yet sweet.

"Wow!" he said. "Definitely worth waiting for. I was smart to let you grow up."

If I had been one ounce less strong, I'd have pushed the papers off my desk and have had at him right there. But Cotter's Corner is too small a town to tolerate the gossip an act like that would have generated. I stood strong. After all, I was at work.

"I have a beautiful Mercedes in the shop. How about I pick you up after work and show it to you before we go to dinner? I'll take you to Le Noir."

"I love that restaurant." I didn't mention that the last time I'd been there I'd been with Yates.

"I'll call later with the final details. Hug Messy for me," he smiled. "I'll hug you later."

No Scoop when the door flew open a few minutes later. "Hi, Lacy, I was going to call you." I looked up from the paper and caught sight of her face, one side was a mass of bruises; her eye looked half destroyed. "My god! What happened?" I rushed to hug her but she pushed me away and sat down.

"If you tell anyone what I'm going to tell you," she said, her lips swollen and contorted, "I'll never speak to you again."

"It was Trey, wasn't it? I knew he was no good. It was Trey, right?"

"Promise you'll keep your mouth shut. Sam, I don't want to read about this in your column." She tried to laugh but it obviously hurt too much.

"Promise." *How could I keep such a promise when my friend was so battered?*

"It wasn't all Trey's fault, not really. I made him furious. We'd been having trouble. That's why I didn't call. I knew you'd tell me to dump him, and I thought he and I cared enough about each other to work it out."

"Lacy, your face looks like a melon that's been gone at with a baseball bat. Don't you dare tell me this was your fault."

"Does it really matter whose fault it was? What matters is that Trey and I are through. I did stop in to see one of my aunt's renters who was an RN. She told me what to pick up at the drugstore and what to look for in case infection sets in or my eye starts giving me trouble."

"Sweetie, I still think I should take you to the doctor. We could go to prompt care in Grand Rapids. No one would have to know."

"The nurse told me that these things frequently look worse than they are. Could I stay with you for a few days and stay out of sight? Jenny's going to pick up some extra shifts and help out."

I just bet, I thought to myself. But Jenny is a victim, too, I remembered. Trey uses women. He always has.

"Stay as long as you want. It's just Messy and me." *And Charley*. I wasn't sure what I'd do with him.

"Let's get you home and to bed. Do you want me to take you?"

"I'm fine. I really feel normal. I don't want to scare anyone, though. That's the only reason I'm going to lie low for a little while."

"Here are the keys. Messy is there and will guard you. Get to bed. The upstairs guest room is all set."

"I'm not that tired. I might just watch old movies and eat. I picked up some food from the restaurant for us for the next couple of days." She took the keys and gave me a hug. "We've been through a lot together, girl. Here's one more chapter."

"Here's to the start of a brand new, better chapter."

I called Aggie who assured me she'd head to my house. "I was going to have lunch with Cat, but I'll tell her what's happened. She'll understand."

"Promise her that you won't call the police on Trey. I think she'll bolt if she thinks we'll betray her."

"Sure." Aggie said. "I've had friends go through this. I know what to do."

Scoop surfaced an hour later.

"You missed all the excitement," I said. "Where were you?"

"You think I have to give you the details of my life?"

"I do. Lacy was here, all beaten up by Trey. She's at my house while he gets his badass self out of hers."

"Hope you told her to get herself to the police."

"Right. Think about it. What's wrong with your logic?"

"She could go to the county sheriff."

"I don't think there's any way you can escape the fact that Trey is a cop and cops stick together."

"Did she need to go to the hospital?"

"She says she had someone check her out, but she looks so bad, Scoop. He really socked her."

"The shit!"

"Sure is."

"I hear that Leland has been calling your mother."

"That's probably the most awkward change of topics I've experienced. First we're talking about Lacy getting battered, and then you're talking about my mother's ex."

"It was a harmless question." He went to the empty coffee pot. "Don't you ever make coffee?"

"I've been getting mine at Octane to Go, but I didn't even do that today. My nerves are jangled enough. You should cut back too."

"Is he calling a lot?"

"Leland? Not that I know of, but now that we're asking questions, I'm going to ask you one. You don't have any thoughts about reconciling with Mother, do you?"

He looked like a deer in the headlights. "I'm not sure it's any of your business."

"It's totally my business. Your marriage messed up my life. I've run from marriage thinking mine would be like the one my mother had."

"Since you're getting all warm and fuzzy, I'll tell you that I know that ship has sailed. I'm not going to risk carving away at her life again. I don't like Leland Henry, though, never did. Hell, I was too old for her so he sure is. And he's a snob."

"And you know this how?"

"I know this because every summer that you were here, he called me to try to let him send you to one of those noses-in-the-air snob camps. He always became furious when I refused. Luckily, your mother didn't fight me."

"I never knew that."

"Now you do, and it doesn't change a thing."

"Whether you like him or not, he took good care of us. He saw to it that I had everything I needed and more. His money even helped me buy into this paper and save your hide."

"I'm not saying he's the devil. I just said I don't like him, and I don't like him for her."

"I don't want to hurt your feelings, Scoop, but I don't get the idea that Mother's going to ask you what you think is good for her."

"I know. I had my chance and I blew it."

"She's changed, hasn't she?" I was tired of fighting with him. "In Chicago all her friends were rich and boring. It's like she's a new person here."

"Not new, just resurfaced," he smiled and across his face was memory mixed with regret. It was almost painful to see.

"Aggie said that, too, that Mother was a different woman when she was young."

Scoop's face and voice softened simultaneously. "She was young and hopeful and, I suppose, in love. When we were first married, she sewed everything from curtains to my shirts. And then, and it's no secret, you came along a few months later. She knit and sewed for you. I think she liked doing those things. When she didn't like was waiting all hours of the day and night for me to show up." It was the first time in my life I'd ever seen a look cross Scoop's face that might most accurately be described as credibly remorseful.

"You were a rat." Remorse or no remorse, I wasn't going to trip along gaily on his half truths. He'd made my mother's life miserable.

"I was a big rat. And your mother took a lot of crap before she took you and bolted for greener pastures. She was too young, but I was younger—emotionally. And there was no excuse. I'd already been married a couple of times. I should have known better." He looked old.

"She had a poor life with you and a rich life with Leland. She wasn't happy in either one. But maybe you each tried in your own way."

"Maybe. So I hear she's gone out with Geof Mapes." He referred to the recently divorced doctor the town would probably dub its most eligible male over sixty.

"She's dated him among others," I said nonchalantly. "She's kind of the belle of the ball, but I don't think she's ready to be serious about anyone. You say you don't have any plans to get her back, then why are you at her house every time I turn around?"

"Two old friends watching *Now Voyager* and falling asleep. Harmless. How about we change the subject?"

"All right," I said. "I've been playing around again with the idea that all three murders and Charles Senior's suicide are in some way related. My cleverness, however, has come up with exactly nothing."

"My mind has been ping ponging similar thoughts," Scoop tapped his pen on his desk. "The only thread I have is very loose. Elli used to sell her bread at Cotter Manufacturing once a week. Mabel worked for Cotter during her early years of trying to get ahead in business. Burt was a janitor there before they sent him to jail for stealing from the workers. He might have gone to prison if Charles, Sr., hadn't interceded."

"You're right. It's a stretch. Most everyone in this town has some connection to Cotter."

"Maybe, but I'm not letting go of it yet," he said.

"One of the questions I can't resolve," I said, "is whether or not the three murders in some way triggered Mr. Cotter's suicide. What do you think?"

"I can't see how it plays into the mix." He poured himself a cup of newly-brewed but dangerous-looking coffee. "Cotter was depressed for decades. He'd been seeing a psychiatrist, but the town kept it quiet. I heard that he'd just had his medication increased. With antidepressants, that's not always a good idea. Hey, I had some papers on my desk." He suddenly noticed the stack I'd moved to my desk.

"I'll get them for you. I edited copy and checked accounts."

"You might get a raise."

"You can't afford it," I laughed. "Remember, I do your books."

Scoop ran a couple of errands, set type and then decided to get a haircut. "I'll be back to close up. Why don't you knock off early?"

"I think I will. I'm going to dinner with Charley."

"Charley again?" He shook his head. "He's not the guy for you."

"And that would be because?"

"Because he has a track record that ain't great. Past is prologue, my darling daughter."

"Let's make a deal. You don't comment on my dates, and I'll force myself to keep quiet about yours."

"Even if I date your mother?" He winked wickedly.

"You said you had no intention of doing that."

"But you know what a liar I am."

"Don't."

"Don't you either." He stared at me, but I stared right back without blinking.

Scoop left, and I called Charley to let him know I'd be ready at home at six and stopped at The Ample Spoon to pick up Annette Stancati's fabulously rich and tasty pizza for Lacy and Aggie, as well as a large antipasto salad and chocolate tiramisu. Along with the food Lacy had provided, that should hold all of us for a few days.

Aggie and Lacy were watching *The Texas Chainsaw Reunion,* or something like that, when I walked in. Messy was between them on the couch in the TV room.

"Aggie has shown me how to figure out the quilt pattern." Lacy's face was still a mess, but her mood had lightened considerably. "She might get me sewing yet. Aunt Mabel left me a fairly new sewing machine."

"You're going to have everyone in town quilting." I smiled at Aggie as I put the pizza, salads, and desserts in front of them. "There's pop and water in the fridge," I said. "Will you two be all right if I go out for a couple of hours?"

"We're fine. I have three movies with me." Aggie took a piece of pizza with cheese that trailed after it. "I also brought a suitcase if you have a place for me to stay."

"Great! I'll change the sheets in the downstairs guest room before I go."

"Nonsense," Aggie said as Messy sniffed her pizza. "I know where everything is. Lacy and I can make a bed."

"I do think we can manage that." Lacy was already on her second piece of pizza.

"Then I think I'll get ready." I watched Messy dance around both my friends begging for handouts. "Look at you!" I petted her. "You are better!"

"Oh, she is," Lacy smiled. "You should see her chase the squirrels in the backyard. I think they're surprised and a little terrified at how quickly she's recovered."

I hugged my dog and raced upstairs to be ready for Charley. I took a quick shower, and decided on a very hot red silk dress and five inch heels. I'd still be shorter than him, and I wanted to take his breath away.

Charley rarely saw me dressed up. I wanted tonight to be different.

The phone rang and I was sure it was Charley saying he'd be early. It wasn't. "I can't believe it's actually you." Yates Logan's unwelcome voice responded to my "hello."

"Yates. I'm in a hurry."

"I wanted to tell you that I'm winding up some business in the next few days and will stop to see you before I go back to Chicago."

"I thought I made it pretty clear that we have nothing to say to each other."

"Sam, we were friends and lovers for over three years, certainly you can at least give me a cup of coffee or a glass of wine. I want to see."

"Okay." There are women hard-hearted enough to respond to Yates' plea with a firm "no!" but I wasn't one of them.

"Great. I'll call when I'm about half an hour out," he said.

I gave him my cell number, said goodbye, and concentrated on the much happier thought of seeing Charley very soon.

I took one last look in the mirror before going downstairs to answer the ringing doorbell. Not bad. I'd lost the couple of pounds I'd put on between Yates and Charley. And my legs were still long and shapely. I would probably never be on the cover of Vogue, but I might still turn a few heads. I hoped I could always turn Charley's. He could certainly turn mine.

"Beautiful," he said half an hour later as he ran his hands up and down my arms. "I've made it clear that I can't take my eyes off you, haven't I?"

"I think so. And you're not looking so bad yourself." He looked GQ perfect in a dark sports coat and slacks with a salmon shirt and darker salmon-colored tie. His hair was perfectly brushed back, with that errant strand falling casually and effectively just above one of his heat-seeking eyes.

"We're leaving," I shouted to Aggie and Lacy, but whatever slasher flick had their attention was blasting so loudly that they didn't hear me. How could they, given what had been going on in town for the last month, even consider watching a bloodcurdling flick?

"I can't get over you in that dress," Charley had ushered me into one of his many little sports cars. It was small so our shoulders were touching. "By the way, we're doing some very messy painting at the shop so I thought we'd put off a visit until after Christmas."

"Perfect." Everything was perfect. His after-shave was a symphony of all the right smells. I'd better settle down or we wouldn't make it to dinner.

"Looks crowded," I said as we pulled into Le Noir's parking lot. "I hope you made reservations."

"Not to worry," he assured me. "We'll get in. I own part of this place."

"Really?" I knew the Cotters owned most of the town but didn't think that meant restaurants, too.

"This way." He put his hand on my back and led me through the crowd to a romantic, candle-lit corner. The restaurant, as elegant as any I'd frequented in Chicago, caters to the lake crowd and closes January through March. It's everyone's favorite place for a special evening.

"When Leland and my mother visited, they brought me here. I never had a bad meal," I said as I studied the menu.

"Did I ever tell you how happy I was to hear that you were moving to town?" Charley loosened his tie and put his hand over mine. "It was the damndest thing. We'd hardly ever spent any time together, but when I heard that Samuels Hayes had bought into her father's newspaper, my heart did a flip."

"I bet."

"No, it did. It was as if I'd been waiting for you."

"You did save me from drowning that summer after my sophomore year. And you know that some cultures believe if you save a life, then you're responsible for it."

"Wouldn't I love to have that duty," he leaned in and kissed my cheek. "I wish my father were alive to see how my taste in women has improved."

All I could do was smile. It was as if we were in one of those movies where everyone disappears except the two lovers. It happened in the dance scene with Darcy and Elizabeth in the Keira Knightly *Pride and Prejudice*. I loved that moment in the movie but didn't believe it happened in real life. And yet here I was. All the tables and people disappeared to leave me alone with Charley. No murders, no doubts—just Charley and me.

"Are you ready to order?" The smiling server was back, along with all the other people in the room.

"Give us a couple more minutes, please." Charley asked. "I'm a little afraid about all this," Charley said as soon as the server left.

"All what?"

"I'm risking everything on the chance that I can be who you need me to be. I got tired of the old me. Frankly," he laughed, "I think a lot of people did."

"Don't get rid of old Charley entirely. Just lose the part that wanted lots of women."

"I'm not sure it was about wanting a lot of women," he whispered. "It was more about knowing there was someone out there for me but never finding her. I had to keep looking."

"Wow! That's the best rationale for womanizing I think I've ever heard."

"I love that song," Charley changed the subject and looked toward the orchestra.

"It's the theme from *Picnic*," I said. "I love it too."

He rose. "How hungry are you?"

"I can wait."

He led me to the dance floor where a few other couples were moving to the slow, smooth melody. And then I was in his arms, being led strongly and confidently around the room. All those years of dances in high school and college had not prepared me for the physical and emotional impact of being held by Charley as an orchestra played just for us, or so it seemed.

"This was a good idea," his breath was warm against my cheek.

"Great idea." I leaned against him until it felt as if we were one person floating over the dance floor.

"We either get a room or get our minds off getting a room by getting something to eat," Charley said when the music stopped and we returned to our table. "You continue to surprise me."

"Me, too, you."

Though I could hear my mother's voice in my head saying, "Be a lady, order fish." I ordered the Kobe beef with a wine reduction. Charley had prime rib.

"I'm going to be gone for a few days," he said. "It's the last long trip I make to Chicago and it's unavoidable. I'm bringing the new Cotter Foundation CEO back with me. He's an old friend, and he'll be great at this job. I'll be back Saturday. Save it for me."

"Done." This time I took his hand.

"Look who just walked in." Charley looked past me to a handsome couple approaching us.

I nearly failed to recognize Scoop. My mother was her usual knockout self. Scoop was the shocker. Now I knew why he'd left the office early. His hair was newly cut. Gone was the ponytail. Instead, his gray hair looked thicker and more lustrous, cut just under his ears and slicked back. He looked almost elegant in a tweed jacket and brown slacks. For the first time in my life, I got a glimpse of the man my mother fell in love with.

My mother had most of the men in the room looking her way. She was in a wine-colored dress that emphasized the breasts Leland had paid to refurbish a few years before. And the short, short dress displayed her legs, showing that the many yoga and Pilates workouts paid off. Her hair was swept into a casually elegant updo. She was radiant, and Scoop couldn't take his eyes off her. She, however, had hers on me. She looked as if she were caught with her hand in the cookie jar. When Scoop finally turned to see what or who she was looking at, he, too, looked stunned that I was there with Charley.

"Hello," my mother was cool as a cucumber. "You didn't tell me you were going to be here."

"Ditto." I responded.

"You both look so lovely," she said to Charley and me.

"You certainly don't look like anyone's mother," Charley, ever gracious, saved the day.

"Would you like to join us?" my mother asked.

"No," Scoop jumped in. "Cat, they don't want to hang with the parents."

"Right." My father had probably never been more right. If I weren't so happy to have Charley there, I would be apoplectic that they, who'd just assured me they were only friends, had the unmistakable tint of reunited lovers.

"Then we'll see you at home," my mother drifted off with Scoop in tow.

"They always say to look at the mother when you want to know how the daughter will turn out. I'd say I'm one lucky boy."

"This steak is delicious." I was done talking about my parents.

It was easy to forget my parents' appearance when Charley and I were together. We ate and danced. I could have foregone the eating and just danced.

"Dessert?" he asked when we returned to the table.

"Order something for me," I said. "I need to run to the powder room."

"*Crème brûlé* it is. Remind me to bring Jersey here."

"Jersey?" I asked as rose to leave.

"He's the new head of The Cotter Foundation. We were roommates at prep school and for a year of college. He was a kid from the projects on full scholarship and the smartest, nicest guy you'll ever meet. His name is Malachi White, but he's from Newark so everyone called him Jersey. It stuck."

"It will be nice to meet a friend of yours from your misspent youth," I kidded him as I left for the rest room.

The ladies room was all diffused lighting, floral smells, and gold trimmed walls. I wanted to hurry to get back to Charley so I took only a minute to look around.

I'd finished and was washing my hands in the sink when I heard someone walk up behind me. "I'll be done in a minute," I said as I ran my hands under the dryer.

Instead of a "thank you" from the person to whom I spoke, my hair was jerked back so hard it felt as if my scalp was being ripped off. Then a hand shoved my head down as the other one put its thumb in that little spot between your neck and collar bone that can take you to your knees. And, in my case, someone was exerting great pressure. The pain was excruciating.

Duct tape was slammed over my mouth and wrapped so tightly around my hands that they tingled from lack of circulation. I was punched in the ribs, and before I could straighten up, I was shoved into a stall and my head was plunged into a toilet. I kicked and gyrated frantically, but my head remained submerged. My attacker was stronger, meaner, and brutally determined. I was going to suffer the ignominious fate of being drowned in a toilet. No Charley. No future. Panic and desperation sank into the water with me. I wanted the terror to be over. The hands pushed my head against the bottom of the toilet. I was floating above it all, watching myself being murdered. Murdered. The agony would be over soon, and I would be the fourth victim of the Cotter's Corner killer. But why?

Chapter Twelve

"C'mon, baby, c'mon. That's a girl." Charley's voice sounded far off and desperate. There was another sound, a choking sound—my choking sound.

Charley's hands pushed against my chest, and his mouth was breathing into mine. "Oh, thank God!" I heard him say. "She's breathing."

"Sam, dear Sam," my mother was on her knees beside me crying. "We thought we'd lost you." Scoop was now next to her, holding her and me alternately, and, I think, he was crying, too."

When I opened my eyes, I saw a small crowd around us—people I didn't know. Charley stroked my hair and repeated, "Baby."

My throat hurt and my ears throbbed. Slowly I remembered the horror of being held under water. Slowly I recognized that someone had just tried to murder me.

The restaurant manager insisted that I go by ambulance to be thoroughly examined by a doctor. I hate hospitals and fought going, but in the end, Charley's saying, "Sam, I'm not risking anything going wrong. I almost lost you," won out.

The doctor checked me out and within an hour, I was at Charley's. "You're staying at my house," he insisted, and my parents didn't object. "I'm going to keep you safe."

"He's private security. We use him other places but I'm having him look after you," Charley said when I asked why the policeman was in front of his house. "It makes sense until we find out who did this to you and why. There's another guard at your house, watching over Lacy and Aggie, and Messy, of course. The sheriff will be here tomorrow."

"The sheriff?"

"I called her. It's time someone other than Trey took over." Charley was helping me get undressed.

"No one ever looked that good in one of my t-shirts," he smiled approvingly as I pulled the shirt he'd given me over my head.

"Are you going to sleep here too?" I teased as Charley tucked me into bed.

"You bet," he said sliding in next to me. He was fully clothed, but not for long. Who knew that for me a near death experience would be a total turn on!

****

Everyone was up by the time I walked downstairs. My head was undeniably a conglomeration of terror and ecstasy. I would concentrate on the ecstasy because I had no idea how to deal with the terror.

I wasn't sure, given how late it was by the time we got to sleep, how Charley managed to be making waffles and sausage, but a plate was waiting for me when I walked into the kitchen. "The sheriff will be here in half an hour," he winked at me as he skillfully served up the waffles.

My relief at not having to deal with Trey quickly dissipated as I recognized how much like him the sheriff was. Her Royal Bossypants didn't like me at all. I could tell by the snotty way she posed her questions. "How do you know you were attacked?" she of the comfortable shoes and wide girth intoned.

"Her head was shoved into a toilet," Charley snapped. "How's that for an indicator?"

'If you don't mind," the woman shot him a "shut up" scowl, "I'll ask Ms. Hayes the questions and talk to you when I'm done with your girlfriend, okey dokey?"

"Go ahead," I said, not wanting the woman to hear what I was sure Charley was about to say.

"Did you know the so-called attacker?" she asked.

"I didn't see the attacker," I tried to remain composed. "I was washing my hands at the sink when I was grabbed from behind."

"So you don't know if it was a man or a woman?"

"I think a man. The person seemed strong."

"So you don't think women can be strong?" The sheriff bristled.

"What does that have to do with anything?" Now I was getting mad.

"Let's do this another way." She tried to smooth her too-tight polyester pants. "How much did you have to drink last night?"

"Are you suggesting that this is all a figment of my drunken imagination?" Rage burned my ears.

"I'm not suggesting anything," she gave me her eat-shit-and-die stare. "I'm asking important questions. If you would answer them quickly, then we can see what's going on."

"I had a glass of wine." I couldn't look at her.

"Do you always drink that much?"

"A glass of wine? Are you kidding me!" I stood.

She stood. "I caution you, Ms. Hayes, insubordination could cost you a night in jail."

This was becoming farcical. "All I can say," I hissed, "is that I can see why no progress has been made in the murder investigations." Now I shot her my version of an eat-shit-and-die stare, the one reserved for cheating boyfriends and boring college professors.

She was silent so I continued my line of questioning. "If you're saying that I had so much to drink that I rushed to a toilet, stuck my head in it, and tried to drown myself, perhaps you should consider another occupation. Last night was terrifying and awful, and I'd like to know who did it, if you don't mind."

My fury must have emanated from every pore because the sheriff visibly backed down. "This was probably a random attack," she relaxed her tone.

"I hear that a lot around this town. It's starting to wear thin. This little town had had one murder in decades. Now murder is nearly a weekly occurrence." My tone remained not-so-relaxed.

"I've been busy and haven't been involved with the murders. I do stay in touch with Chief Davis who tells me he has several leads. He and I are old friends from the police academy. I know he's a super trouper."

He's a pooper trouper, and you are too, I thought. *Scoop and I have a greater chance of solving the murders than you two stooges.*

But the fact that she and Trey were old friends explained why she couldn't stand me. Thanks to he of the low IQ and high self-esteem, the press on me had not been good.

"I'll look into this," she walked toward the foyer without looking at me, "but I think it's nothing more than you were in the wrong place at the wrong time."

It's more like you're in the wrong job at the wrong time.

"I'm going to stop in to see Chief Davis on my way home. I'll inform him about your attack and see what progress he's making on the murders."

"You think the murders are connected, though, don't you?" I asked.

"Neither Chief Davis nor I see a direct connection between victims. And we've had much more experience with these kinds of things than the random citizen." She glared at me.

I pulled rank. "Well, the state police have kept us apprised of what's going on, and they don't think a connection is out of the question."

"This is our case, not theirs." She stomped out the door and slammed it. Sheriff Paula Ziemba was not a fan.

"That was unpleasant. I'm going to see if we can't find someone to run against her in the next election." Charley entered the room as soon as Sheriff Ziemba left.

"She didn't believe me," I disparaged. "She's a friend of Trey's."

My mother arrived as Charley left for the airport.

"Take care of her," he said as if he were the parent. "She's not as fully recovered as she claims."

"You do look amazingly good for someone who nearly disappeared from our world last night," my mother sat next to me. "I couldn't live if something happened to you."

"Am I allowed to ask what was going on with you and Scoop last night? I thought you told me you were just friends." I didn't want to talk about what had happened to me. I needed time to fully process how close to being the fourth victim I'd been.

"Friends with benefits. Isn't that what the kids call it?" My mother was in a teasing mood.

"Has Leland's divorcing you pushed you over the edge? Scoop? Are you insane?"

"Haven't you heard there's a thin line between love and hate?" She studied her perfectly manicured nails. "I've loved/hated your father since the day I met him. At first there was more love than hate. Then there was a bucket load more hate than love. Now I'd say it's pretty even."

My head hurt, and my mother wasn't making it better. "Well, it sounds pretty nuts to me. The man has spent most of the past twenty years dating women half your age and a third your IQ. Is this really someone you can have a relationship with?"

"We'll see." She put her hands on my shoulders. "Sam, you and I have spent so many years playing it safe, making sure we don't lose our footing. Maybe a mother shouldn't say this to her daughter, but I think once in a while it's good to be a little off balance. Haven't the murders in this town taught us that life is too short to waste it worrying about the future? What if there isn't one?"

"I can't talk to you about this. I'm wondering who you are and what you've done with my mother."

"I just took a phone call, someone named Jivy, I think." Lacy was a welcome break from arguing with my mother.

"Jersey?" I asked.

"Who's that?" My mother was always on a need-to-nose-in basis.

"It's a friend of Charley's who's coming to head the foundation. What did he want?"

"He was trying to catch Charley to tell him that Chicago is fogged over so he might want to rethink taking off for a while. They're expecting a big snowstorm later too. I guess he couldn't get Charley on his cell."

"They'll tell him the situation at the airport," my mother said.

"Whatever his name is, he sounds cute." Lacy kept her voice low so my mother, who was getting ready to leave, wouldn't hear.

Lacy went back to bed about a half an hour later so I followed her lead and left Aggie in the kitchen drinking coffee and reading *Life and Love Weekly* while I went upstairs to try to get more sleep.

Messy was lying next to me in the bed I'd shared with Charley just hours before when a wave of panic flooded me. The sheriff and the others in the house had kept me from thinking about my near-death experience. Now all by myself, with almost total recall of the previous night, I was shaking all over.

Chapter Thirteen

The next few days were spent working from home with the security guard posted in front of my house. Lacy's face healed enough to make it look like the bruising was a result of some rough dental work, so she went back to work. A few days before the attack, I'd had another note from the Internet syndicate interested in a blog, so today was the day I was going to put something together.

Truthfully, I was excited about doing some legitimate writing that might lead to something on a more national level. Since the murders had already called attention to my adopted hometown, why not write something *à la* Dominic Dunne, only on less elegant scale. He'd already done society murders in Connecticut. I might be the new chronicler of less high class murders in Michigan. After all, in its own way, Cotter's Corner had as much caché and charisma as any little town in Connecticut.

I emailed Hometown Treasures, the name of the syndicate, to let them know I'd have something for them the first of the year. Then for the next few hours, I roughed out some blog entries about my murder series which would be called Home Sweet Homicide.

After working on the blog and playing with Messy, I was at thoroughly loose ends. I didn't want to sew, and certainly had no interest in ripping open the new machine and spending hours learning how to work its elaborate self.

I grabbed Messy's leash. "C'mon, girl! We're going to walk to see Lacy and get a latté." No furry dog in sight. "I'll get you a cookie." Out of nowhere Messy appeared, took her leash in her mouth, and headed to the door.

Ever since elementary school lunch when I laughed so hard milk ran out my nose causing all my classmates to laugh hysterically and point at me, I have hated being the center of attention. It was crystal clear, though, there was no way I could avoid it today. Cars slowed to look at the woman who nearly drowned in the toilet. The man who held the door for me at Mabel's told me how glad he was to see me alive. Good news travels fast in Cotter's Corner. Bad news travels even faster.

"I'm going to make you a sandwich and give you a real fountain Coca Cola," Lacy said, dark glasses covering up most of Trey's damage. "I'm so glad to see you. Hey, I saw someone drive by with Charley."

"Chloe?" It was out of my mouth before I could stop it.

"No, silly girl. I think it was that Jivy fellow that Charley mentioned a while ago. I saw him only from a distance, but he's one great looking black man."

"And his being black is important because?"

"Because my mother was black and my father was white. For some reason, the men I've dated have been white. That hasn't worked out so well. Maybe I need to change teams."

"His name is Malachi White but they call him Jersey. I hope he's someone worthy of you."

"Even if it doesn't work out, he's pretty darn cute, even from a distance."

"I don't know whether or not he's married," I said, relieved that Charley had a same-sex passenger, "but let's hope he's not. How are you explaining those dark glasses?"

"Pink eye if anyone asks."

"You're kidding? Aren't you worried customers will turn and run?"

"I tell them I've been on antibiotics, and that I'm no longer contagious."

"I think I'd still be afraid to have you serve me food."

"Thanks a lot."

"Want to watch old movies tonight?"

"I think I'm going to go home after work and go to bed. I had all the locks changed and Scylla looks scary even if she's a cream puff."

"Since you're no fun, I think I'll concentrate on seeing who put my head in the toilet."

"You're kidding, right? I mean, you're not going to go near anyone who might be dangerous?"

"Maybe. Maybe not."

"You're scaring me," Lacy said. "You sound like you used to when we played girl detective at The Mill Pond. You know this isn't playing make believe, don't you? You are aware that people die."

I assured Lacy I was well aware of the dangers involved in getting in too deep. When she laughed, I realized she was thinking about my experience with the toilet. "I didn't mean to make fun of what happened last night," I said.

I got home just in time to greet Yates Logan at my back door. "Yates, I thought you were going to call."

"Aren't you going to invite me in?" He opened the screen door so that I'd have little choice except to let him enter.

"I finished early and am going to catch a plane out of Grand Rapids in a couple of hours so I thought I'd surprise you."

"You have." I had no idea what I was going to say so when the front doorbell rang again, I viewed it as a stay of execution.

"I came over to see how . . . oh, hello, Yates." It was one of the first times I remember seeing my mother caught awkwardly off guard. "Sam, you didn't tell me Yates was visiting. I wouldn't have dropped in."

"She didn't know, Mrs. Henry. I surprised her."

"That's right. He did." I was stuck for words and struck by how handsome a man Yates Logan is. In my frustration over his mild-mannered, sycophantic ways, I had overlooked his exceptional good looks. He stands militarily straight and he's appealingly tall, a man who's made for exquisitely-tailored suits. He would have been the perfect package if the box hadn't been empty.

"How about if I make us some coffee?" My mother seemed as unnerved by Yates' appearance as I was.

"Good idea!" I was so glad my mother was staying around. "Let's go into the family room," I said, noticing Messy, leash still dangling, who was weaving in and out of Yates' legs. My dog was making him obviously uncomfortable.

"Never was too crazy about dogs," he said, pulling his hand away so Messy couldn't lick.

He's prissy, I thought as I waved Messy away from him—another reason I didn't want him around on a permanent basis.

"Too bad about your mother and Leland," he said after seconds of awkward silence.

"Oh, that's old news for her. You know how it is, nothing lasts forever."

"I know he has regrets, Sam, real regrets."

That's why you're here, you jerk. You came to plead Leland's case. "He needs to move on," I said. "When something is over, it's over."

"We're not talking just about Leland, are we?" He took off his suit coat and placed it on the antique rocker by the fireplace. "I can't for the life of me figure out why you have so coldly kicked me to the curb. What do I have to do to get another chance?"

"It's not about second chances, Yates. You know as well as I do that we weren't totally crazy about each other and that's what I want—crazy."

"I am crazy about you. I just don't go all weak-kneed and soppy."

As Yates stepped toward me, I stepped back, nearly tripping over Messy. Fortunately the doorbell again saved me.

"Look who's here," my mother answered the door and stepped aside so Charley could enter the room.

"Hi, darling," he said taking me into his arms like Rhett took Scarlett or Harry took Sally.

"Oh, I'm sorry," he stopped to acknowledge Yates. "Cupcakes and I have been apart for at least twelve hours, and I can't bear it." He kissed me again.

Yates looked like he'd kill Charley if he could. "How long has this been going on?" he stared at the floor.

"Since we were sixteen?" Charley laughed. "First puppy love and then full-out love. Right, sweet cheeks?" He put his arm around me.

"This is a pretty low blow." Yates now looked at me full out with more hurt than hate in his eyes. I felt terrible.

"Yates, Charley's kidding."

"Right. I saw that kiss. I won't be bothering you anymore." He grabbed his jacket, took his topcoat from my mother's waiting hands, and left.

"I don't think he'll be back," Charley said. "Makes me feel a little sorry for him."

"How did you just happen to show up?" I didn't know if I should cheer him or chide him, but I was leaning toward cheer. It would be so nice to have Yates in the past once and for all.

"I called him, from the kitchen," my mother said. "I've given you so much grief over Yates that I thought the least I could do was get Charley over here as fast as I could."

"Good thing I was back in town, huh?" He kept his arm around me.

"Good thing."

"I came over to make sure you're all right. I can see you are so I'm going to go about running some errands." My mother put her fur jacket back on and left.

"Alone at last," Charley said.

"Thanks for being such a good boyfriend," I said, kissing him.

"Good boyfriend had nothing to do with it. I'm a little sick of that guy and wanted to let him know you're my girl. If that first kiss didn't convince him, nothing will. I'm still weak from it. Good job, Sam."

"Anything to please." I kissed him again, not five-alarm but close.

I was about to try to top it, but Aggie was on my iPhone. I let it ring. Then I started thinking that maybe I should have taken her call. "You mind if I call her back?"

"Not one little bit. I'm done rescuing fair maidens for the moment. I need to get back to work. How about if we go for a drink tonight? I'll call you."

One more kiss and then he left me to return Aggie's call.

"Oh, Snoopy, I feel so dumb. I'm such an old mess. When I tell you what I've done, you'll know how useless I am."

"Aggie, honey, you are wonderful everyday of your life. Calm down and tell me what you've done so we can fix it."

"It's not what I've done," she said. "It's what I didn't do."

"Slow down. Breathe deep. I'm on my way." I told Messy to watch the house while I was gone, grabbed my bag with the car keys, raced to Aggie's in the rattling Honda.

Aggie's neighbors peeked out their windows as I drove into her driveway. Her section of town is known as The Flats. It's also less kindly known as The Tracks, as in "other side of." I've offered many times to use some of my idle trust fund money to get Aggie a nicer, safer house. Each time she bristles and tells me not to bring it up again. "I'm not a charity case, and I don't want you spending your money on me," she says. The truth is that she can't bear the thought of leaving her beloved house—the house that she and her cherished husband Tubby spent their time together in.

Tubby, like his father and his father's father, one day parked himself on the railroad tracks. "The family sadness got to him," is the way Aggie describes the bi-polar condition that afflicted Tubby and a large part of his family. She'll sometimes continue by saying, "His whole family seemed to have an unexplained sorrow." So Aggie has babysat, wall-papered, sewn, and played Bingo for thirty some years since Tubby disappeared from her life but not from her heart.

When I got to her front door, she collapsed into my arms. "Snoopy, I am an old, useless woman. I forgot something that might solve Elli's murder. Here it is." In her hands was a wrinkled, large manila envelope. "Oh, please don't hate me for this. It might be nothing. I hope it's nothing because then I'm off the hook. But if it's something and helps find who killed Elli, then I guess I'll have to suffer the consequences of my stupidity."

"Aggie, you're going to give yourself a heart attack. You didn't do anything wrong. I'm sure you didn't. The

world isn't going to explode because of what's in this."
I took the envelope from her trembling hands.

"I hope you're right, Snoopy. Well, I better start at
the beginning so you know how this all came to be.
You know how me and Hilda always wanted Elli's
oatmeal bread recipe. It's the best bread recipe in the
world. In fact, that's its name—The Best Bread Recipe
in the World."

"Aggie, let's get to the point where you think you
did something catastrophic, okay?"

"Okay. Well, Elli absolutely refused to share her
recipe. She said it was a professional secret and her
insurance policy, that she could sell it for a fortune if
she came to needing money. At first I was damn mad
that she wouldn't share it, but one night me and Elli had
a talk and several drinks and decided our friendship was
too important to have a little thing like a bread recipe
come between us. And, besides, how in the hell did the
old bat think her bread was so good people would pay a
fortune for it!"

"The point, Aggie. Let's get to the point."

She took a deep breath. "Okay. Here it is. About six
months ago, Elli just showed up at my door. She
usually phones, but she didn't phone that day. She had
that!" She pointed to the envelope in my hand. "She
told me that she still wouldn't share the bread recipe,
not yet. She also made me promise that I'd hold onto
that envelope and not open it. That's the part I must
have heard, not the other part."

"What other part?"

"The other thing she told me was—and these are her
exact words, I think. She said, 'You can't open it until
after I'm dead and gone.' She wanted me to wait and
open it after she died. How could I have forgot that?
Snoopy, how could I have missed that? I'm just an old,
washed up, idiot of a woman."

"Aggie, that's all? That's what you're upset about? For goodness sake, it happened six months ago. I can't remember what happened a week ago. We all forget things. It's not a crime, and it's certainly no sin." I knew my last point would be the most comfort to the Bible-believing Aggie. "Now, tell me what's inside this."

"Okay. I don't know. I was so afraid of what might be inside that I waited for you so you could open it. What if there's a picture of her murderer?"

"I seriously doubt that. In fact, I doubt it's anything more than the bread recipe, but let's see." I tore the envelope open and pulled out a fairly thick stack of papers. A recipe card fell to the floor.

"Here it is! Here's the recipe!" Aggie danced around as if she'd just found a million dollars. "Wait until I tell Hilda." She started toward the phone.

"Let's see what else is here before you tell Hilda the good news." I flipped through a formal-looking document. At first none of what I read made any sense. Then a name jumped out at me: *Robert Pickett.* A closer look told me that the papers were his prison records. Why would Elli have a copy of Lacy's father's prison records?

"Oh, my lord!" Aggie said as she looked over the papers. "Why did Elli have this? Robert Pickett was a devil of a man. This must be the record of his first stay in prison. Yep. I can see by the dates that that's exactly what they are."

"Why would Elli want you to keep these? Is there something about Lacy's dad that you know and I don't?" I tensed, fearing the worst, whatever that was.

"Let's have a drink." Aggie poured her usual tumbler of Jack and a much smaller one for me.

"Aggie?"

"The truth is that only a few of us know what I'm about to tell you. Hilda knows. Mabel Pollock knew, and one or two others knew, but I didn't think Elli was one of them."

"Knew what?"

"We knew that there was no way that Robert Pickett was Lacy's father. Her mother was pregnant when she married him. She'd conceived Lacy while Robert was in prison the first time—the time Lacy doesn't know about . Lacy only knows about this last time that he was sentenced for killing her mother. He was there earlier, for assault and battery. When Sheila—Lacy's mother—found out she was pregnant, she came crying to me. Hilda, Sheila, and I all worked with her on the assembly line at Cotter Manufacturing. She was terrified and didn't know what to do. Mabel forced her to marry that crud Pickett to give the baby a name. They'd only dated a couple of months before he was sent to prison. I'm sure these papers and their dates prove that there's no way Robert Pickett was Lacy's father. Anyway, in those days they didn't have conjoined, or convivial, or whatever kind of visits they have now."

"Conjugal," I corrected before I asked my question. "Why didn't the biological father marry her?"

"He didn't know she was pregnant. That's what she told us, anyway. She loved him, though, but I think he was a white man and married. That just didn't happen in those days—married white men giving up everything to marry black women. So, she got married and didn't tell Pickett—who was always chasing after her—that she was pregnant. Even the doctor, who rented from Mabel, went along with the lie that the baby was premature. Premature my ass. Lacy weighed over eight pounds when she was born. I think that's when Pickett began to figure he'd been snookered, he began to take his anger out on Sheila. She was beautiful and sweet. The whole thing was tragic."

"And you all kept quiet all these years?"

"You know Lacy. There isn't a prettier or more wonderful person in this town, except my Snoopy, of course," she hugged me and then poured more booze.

"I think we need coffee." I went for the Keurig I'd given her at Christmas. We need to be sober to work with this new info. As I spoke, I realized that there was something else in the envelope so I pulled it out.

"It's a copy of a deed to the old Trainor farm. I'd heard it was for sale. My gosh. Look at the new owner!" I pointed to the signature at the bottom of the first page: Trey Davis.

"Wow!" Aggie sneaked a little JD into her coffee. "I'd heard his mother left him money when she died. And I couldn't quite figure that out because his family never seemed to have much. I mean, the only job I ever knew Charlotte Davis to have was ironing for other people. Oh, I guess she did some house cleaning when things were lean—like we all did. She might have been really good at pinching pennies, but to have enough for Trey to buy the Trainor place, she'd have to have downright squeezed the blood out of every last one of those pennies."

"Aggie, none of this makes sense." I felt a headache coming on, a big one. Instead of clearing anything up, the papers had muddied the waters. I felt farther than ever away from finding the murderer's identity. "I have no idea why Elli would keep Lacy's father's prison papers and a copy of Trey's lease to the farm."

"So you don't think I did something awful by forgetting that Elli left the papers with me?"

"You will always be the dearest person I know. You could never do anything awful. But, sweetie, make sure not to tell anyone, not even Hilda, what we found. And for goodness sake, keep all this stuff where no one will find it." As an afterthought, I added, "but make sure you keep the papers where *you* can find them."

"I can keep the recipe for myself, can't I?" she asked. When I nodded my head, Aggie held the hard won piece of paper to her chest.

"Oh, my mother said to give her a call tomorrow. Your new best friend needs to talk to you." I put away the whiskey. Aggie's face fell. "We've both had enough. Now lock the door after me."

"One more thing," Aggie said.

Oh no, now what?

"Your mother gave me a fantastic new sewing machine. I know I shouldn't have taken it from her, but she wanted to thank me. That's what she said, but I have no idea what she's thanking me for. Do you think I'm wrong to take the machine? She might need the money now that she's divorced."

"Trust me, Aggie, she will not now or ever need the money, and she wanted to get you a new machine. You did a kind thing to take it. And you've made her feel at home here. She considers you a great friend."

I left Aggie with an ear-to-ear grin on her face that I knew was sure to be replaced in a few short hours by a grimace due to the world's biggest hangover.

"I'm staying with you tonight," my mother said. "It will be just like when I visited those weekends after you left Chicago. I'm starving and you have some great food in the fridge."

"It's from Lacy's new Lacy Day Take Out menu. Don't you love the name? She dropped off the food and a copy of the new menu along with lemon bars and milk chocolate brownies."

"Looks mouth watering," she said. "Let me wash up, and then we'll dig in."

"Great. You don't need to stay overnight, though. Charley called when I was on my way home from Aggie's. He'll be here sometime tonight. And the policeman is parked right out front."

"Oh, and here's that raspberry iced tea I love," my mother was still rooting around the fridge.

"Did you hear what I said about Charley?"

"Yeah, he'll make a booty call later."

"Mother!"

My mother stayed until after ten and left only because I assured her Charley would be there any minute.

He called at ten-thirty. "I'm tied up with Jersey. Don't stay up. I know where you keep the key and the police officer knows me, so all's good. Get some sleep."

Trey's in this! It came to me unbidden almost as soon as I'd hung up from talking to Charley. Up until that moment, I'd bought into the theory that Trey's incompetence was why the case was proceeding so unsatisfactorily. Now I saw that it was less incompetence than determination. Trey was determined that no one would ever find out who committed the murders. He'd been paid off. But who would pay to impede the investigation and keep Trey quiet?

As I crawled into bed, with Messy in her bed on the floor beside me, I considered the possibility that Trey had chased after Jenny to get information from her. He was using the shy, naïve girl because of the connection she had to Elli, Burt, and Mabel. I called Scoop, but he had his phone off the hook. I hoped my mother wasn't the reason.

I looked out my window to make sure the policeman was on the street below. He was. I fell into a restful sleep until a figure crawling into bed next to me frightened me awake.

"It's all right, sweetheart." The voice I loved was soft and reassuring. "I'm here, baby." And then Charley wrapped me in his arms. "What would I have done if you'd married the boring guy?" he whispered as I fell asleep.

Morning came way too soon. And how I would have loved to have spent the next day under the covers with Charley, but after a couple of sizzling kisses and eating two of Lacy's delicious sweet rolls, I filled him in on Aggie's find. He was then off to Chicago. "Only a few more days and then I'll pay some real attention to you," he said. "You are mine, you know that, right?"

"I do. Always have been." I put my face in the curve of his neck. "If you don't get going, you'll miss your flight."

"Never have I wanted to miss a flight more, but I have to finish up some loose ends." He got out of bed and turned back to me. "But we could save some time by showering together."

"Love to save time," I said as I raced him to my shower.

An hour later at work, I found myself repeating Aggie's discovery to Scoop. I also shared my newly-forged theory regarding Trey. Scoop wasn't surprised.

"I've been thinking pretty much the same thing, but proving Trey's collusion with the bad guys is another thing," he said as I handed him the sweet roll I'd brought with me for him. "I've known about the Trainor purchase for a while. I admit I fell for the theory that he used money he'd been left by his mother. Only later did I realize that there couldn't have been any money. His dad was a deadbeat and his mother's funeral was paid for by her church. I agree that there's something fishy about Trey, but I can't figure out what."

My last errand was going to be my most difficult. I'd decided not to tell Lacy about finding her father's prison release papers. She'd gotten along without knowing about his first prison stay for a long time, and I hoped she could keep on not knowing it. He may be a jailbird, but he was at least a living, breathing person. I had to believe that not even knowing who your father was would be worse. But there was something else I decided not to keep from her.

I waited until all but one customer was gone before I pulled Lacy aside. "I wasn't going to tell you this, but since I believe you and Trey are forever over, you need to know that I think he's been seeing Jenny Lundy."

"My Jenny?" The look on her fact told me she'd had no idea. "You're sure? I can't believe it." She paused, and then it was if a light had gone on in her brain. "Sam, this explains so much. Jenny has been so secretive and upset lately. She's walked around as if she doesn't know where she is and has been uncharacteristically irresponsible and incompetent. I've had to consider firing her. In fact, I was just about to when she told me she'd be leaving town after the holidays."

"I hope Trey hasn't talked her into thinking she has a future with him. Lacy, I can't help feeling she's in danger. I think Trey has some connection to the murders and that puts Jenny at risk."

She grabbed my wrist. "I know he's capable of bad stuff. Only a couple of times have I seen that temper of his, but it was way too scary to want to see it again."

"Poor Jenny; we have to warn her. Does she come in at all today?"

"No, she has classes. This is the one day she doesn't come in."

"Then I'm going to see if I can catch her at the boarding house."

"I hate to think of that darling little Jenny with someone like Trey." Lacy wrapped her arms around herself. "He's terrible and getting worse."

"Now you know how I felt when you were with him." I hugged her.

I'd been gone long enough that I thought I'd check in at the office before I went looking for Jenny Lundy. The newspaper was locked. Again, I hoped Scoop was off on a legitimate errand and not shacked up with my mother.

He'd left copy on my desk with a note that said, "Please look this over." *Look this over indeed.* It needed a major rewrite so I was there much longer than I wanted to be. I also took time to put Hilda's mouth-watering recipe for buttermilk pie with raspberry topping in *Snooping.* I also threw in her recipe for Congo bars. "They're a hit every time she shares them at Bingo!" Truthfully, they were so sweet they made my teeth ache, but I knew that seeing them in *The Corner News* would give Hilda a boost.

Ding! I was ready to wind up my duties when my email alerted me to two new messages. One was from Rose saying she was feeling far less exhausted and depressed and didn't think she should leave, if even for a short time, to visit Cotter's Corner. She also said she understood my not visiting until spring. I felt bad because I hadn't paid enough attention lately to Rose. Damn murderer!

As if on cue, the second message was cryptic and threatening. "Gossip hurts." When I tried to reply, it came back. I noticed my hands trembled on the keyboard, so I closed everything down and got out of the office.

My life seems to go from bad to worse lately, I thought, as I locked up the office and pointed the Honda toward the boarding house to give Jenny the not-

so-good news that Trey was a skunk and a dangerous
skunk at that.

Chapter Fourteen

"Yes? Can I help you?" She didn't recognize me, but I sure recognized May Abbott, my summer camp crafts teacher. She stood at the door of the center hall colonial she'd turned into a rooms-for-rent boarding house.

"Hello; I'm Samuels Hayes, Scoop's daughter. Remember?"

"Oh, yes." Her expression and tone of voice indicated she definitely remembered the decoupage session during which I'd glued my hand to the object I'd been working on. I still have a little scar inside the thumb of my right hand where the skin came off with the glue when she hysterically worked to free me from my art. "You're the one who had so much trouble with the sewing machine."

I'd forgotten that. She was referring to the several times I either pinched my hand lowering the sewing machine's pressure foot or ran the needle over my finger. More hysteria. "Does Jenny Lundy rent from you?" I asked, tired of the direction the conversation had taken. Couldn't she just have said, "Good to see you?".

"I think she's still home. She got in very late last night." Disdain fell from May Abbott's withered lips. "It's no wonder she's having such a tough time getting through school—too many distractions. Well, I don't mean to gossip. Hers is the second room on the right."

The stairs were many and rickety. I was feeling like it had been too long since I'd been at the gym by the time I knocked on 2 A.

"Come in," a voice whispered. When I entered, Jenny jumped naked from her bed and grabbed a robe draped over a chair near the bathroom. She obviously wasn't expecting me.

"Sam, I'm sorry. I just woke up." Jenny Lundy has that little-girl-lost look that guys fall for, a waif in a woman's body. Lots of eye makeup and freshly applied lip gloss on her rosebud mouth told me that she had *not* been sleeping. What I didn't know was why she told me she had. That sneaky Trey had already had a bad effect on her.

"I'm sorry to just barge in like this," I said as she tied her robe and cleared off two chairs so we could sit down. "I have a few questions that I'm hoping you can answer, though."

"Okay."

"I'm doing some research for an article on Mabel's death. I was wondering if you worked the day of her death."

"Earlier, but I didn't see anything. Mabel was so kind to me, helped me with tuition. I can't imagine anyone wanting to kill her."

I envied Jenny's knowing a kinder, gentler Mabel Pollock. "I know you're a friend of Trey Davis so I wondered if he might have said something to you about the murder."

"No." For an instant, Jenny looked away and then turned her luminous green eyes on me. "I'm expecting someone and since I can't help you, I'll have to ask you to go."

I'm botching it, I thought. *Trey has warned me to keep quiet and I'm blowing any help she might give me.* "You know that they're having trouble solving the murders, right? I thought you could help immensely if there's anything you can remember that connects to Mabel's death."

"Isn't that police business?" Jenny was a hard girl to read.

"You're right. It is. I'm doing some investigative journalism, and if in doing that, I help the police, then all the better. You know, kind of like Woodward and Bernstein. Remember the Watergate scandal?" *How could she remember Watergate? I barely did.*

Her blank stare told me I'd struck rock. Jenny was too young to know what the hell I was talking about.

"Well," I started again. "Two of the murder victims were your relatives."

Her eyes became watery.

"Oh, Jenny, I didn't mean to upset you."

"The police have questioned, and questioned, and questioned me," she sobbed. "I don't know anything. Don't you think if I could come up with one thing that would help the police find the awful person who killed Elli, my dad, and Mabel that I would tell them? The only thing I know is the one thing they didn't seem interested in hearing about. Wesley Falls killed them all, but no one seems to care."

She got my attention. "Who's Wesley Falls?" I'd heard the name somewhere but couldn't remember where.

"He was a friend—a kind of friend—of my dad's. They were in jail together when they were young and stayed in touch. Wes is scary mean. I used to tell Daddy that I didn't like to be around him. Daddy was a good friend, though, and tried to help Wes out. Look what it got him." Tears cascaded down her cheeks.

"You think this Wes Falls murdered your father?"

"Not just Daddy. I think he killed them all. The day Mabel died, Wes was in the restaurant. I'd worked the early-morning shift and was leaving. I bumped into him hanging around the back door. I hurried out the door as fast as I could, but as I left, I could hear Mabel and him screaming at each other."

"You told the police this, and they didn't question him?"

"Oh, they questioned him, but they said he had an alibi. I don't think he did. I think he got someone to lie for him."

"Where does he live?" I was energized by Jenny's newly-supplied information.

"Last I knew he was living with a cousin five miles out of town, but he works at Charley Cotter's car place."

"Wes Falls works for Charley?" That's where I'd heard the name.

"Odd, huh? Charley's dad dies of suicide, or so they say, and then Charley goes and hires Wes Falls." Jenny began to comb her silky blonde hair. "It's all kind of fishy, don't you think?"

I didn't like what Jenny was suggesting. I knew there was no way Charley was involved in anything underhanded, but Wes Falls was another story. Charley might not be aware of the man's past or his connection to Burt. "What do you think was between your father and Wes that might have erupted in violence?" I got the conversation off the Charley track and back on Wes Falls. I couldn't place him, but felt sure once I saw him I'd recognize him.

"He owed Daddy money. I think it was a lot of money. Daddy played the ponies and he had won big. He loaned some of it to Wes. I don't think Wes ever intended to pay it back. That's what Daddy said anyway."

"Jenny, you've been a great help." I left feeling grateful to Jenny and hopeful that I might have some information that could finally solve the murders. I couldn't help wondering why Trey had been so quick to drop the Wes Falls line of questioning.

"Anytime." Jenny smiled, without hesitation slipped out of her robe, revealing a body that any woman would envy. "I think I'll get that nap now." She pulled the covers up over her, and I shut the door behind me. I didn't see what she saw in Trey, but I certainly saw what the older man was attracted to in Jenny Lundy. She was innocent and easy to keep under his thumb, just the way Trey Davis liked 'em.

I feared for a girl so guileless who could easily be sold a bill of goods. Worry over Jenny fed my sense of urgency where solving the murders was concerned. I'd stop at Cotter Restoration before I went home. Charley wouldn't be there, but I hoped someone could guide me toward Wes Falls.

Chapter Fifteen

I stopped at the paper to get my car and drove the three miles on Saw Mill road to Charley's shop. I don't know what I expected but the Cotter Restoration sign, in wood and brass, seemed a bit elegant for a garage. Even more surprisingly elegant were the office and showroom, not a dab of oil or grease in sight. It looked more like an exclusive men's club, all glass and leather, than a car restoration business. Within seconds of my entering his place, the love of my past, present, and hopefully future, walked in.

"You are a dream come true," he kissed me. "I was just this minute thinking about you. I made the pilot fly extra fast so I could get back here to you."

"If I'd known this is the way you greet your visitors, I would have stopped out here a whole lot sooner."

"Let's show you around," he put an arm around me.

"Could I have a tour another time? I didn't come just to see you. I came to see Wes Falls. Does he still work for you?"

"He does." Charley eyed me suspiciously. "But I'm very curious as to why you want to see him. Does it have something to do with the police?"

"No. I just talked with Jenny Lundy and," I lowered my voice, "and she's sure that Wes had something to do with her father's murder. She thinks he killed Mabel and Elli too."

"Did she tell you that he's been totally exonerated by the police?" I could tell that what Jenny had told me had Charley's dander up. "The guy's had nothing but trouble and is working himself to death to pay off old bills. Do you have to bring up such a sore subject?"

"Charley, if he isn't connected, maybe he knows who is. Please let me talk to him."

"Okay, but I wish you wouldn't."

Charley went to find Wes, and I could tell by the way he turned abruptly and left, he was a bit angry.

Within a minute, a man, head bent toward the ground, stood in front of me. Charley stood next to him. "Sam, this is Wes. Wes, this is Sam. I'll leave you two to talk."

"So what do you want?" he snarled. "I'm busy."

"I'm doing a story for the newspaper and wonder if you can tell me a little about your friendship with Burt Lundy."

"Why?" The veins on his neck bulged. "Somebody say something?" He was beet-red ballistic. His pock-marked face looked more through me than at me. "I didn't do nothing wrong. The police put you up to this, didn't they? I told them, and I'll tell you, that me and Burt was friends once, but that was over a long time ago."

"Do you know who might have killed him?" *Was it you?* I struggled to keep from asking.

"Why are you asking me that?" He shouted and then took a threatening step toward me. "You don't have no business coming to where I work and putting your nose in my business."

"Everything Okay, Wes?" Charley had returned and stepped forcefully between us. He was taller than Wes as well as being his boss. Wes Falls became obedient in his presence. "It's all good, Mr. Cotter."

"Great. I thought it was getting loud here, and we have a business to run."

"Yes, sir." He addressed me. "Sorry to get loud. You done with me?"

"I am." Well, Wes Falls had a temper. Was it violent? Could it drive him to murder?

"Are you sure everything is all right?" Charley stepped closer and walked with me out the door.

"I'm fine. Thanks for letting me do this. I didn't mean to upset him."

"He'll be fine. He's tired. All the men are exhausted from the redecorating and also getting a car ready for Pebble Beach. I'm going to let him go home early to get some sleep."

"Wait until I'm out of the driveway, Okay?"

"Sam, are you sure you're all right?"

"I'm just a little tired, that's all."

"Then let's make it a very early night." He pulled me around the side of the building, and gently let both of us fall against it as he pressed against me, letting me dissolve into his kisses.

If Scoop didn't care about work, then I didn't either, I told myself as I drove home. The conversations with Jenny Lundy and Wes Falls had had equally unsettling effects on me. I was wading into danger, a fear of which Charley's kisses couldn't wipe completely away.

The policeman parked in front of the house gave me some reassurance, and Messy's licks helped a little too, but there was still an acknowledgement that I knew a little but not enough. Learning more, however, could be the end of me.

Because I needed something mindless, and because I owed Aggie her quilts, I changed into sweats, let Messy race around the yard with its thin covering of newly-fallen snow, poured a glass of water, and pulled out my piles of half-completed squares. For the next several hours, I thought of nothing but completing the squares. Whenever a thought—any thought—crept into my mind, I smashed it to smithereens. My focus was on the squares, and three hours later, I had them finished and had begun to sew them together. Take that May Abbott!

I was proud of both my mind control and my work so I stopped only when the phone rang, hoping it was Charley saying he was on his way to my eager body. It wasn't.

"This is Wes. I hope it's all right if I call. Mr. Cotter dialed the phone for me so you don't have to worry that I've got your number."

Though his voice at first sent an electric shock through me, his words helped calm me down. "I been trying to keep my nose real clean for a long time. When Burt was murdered, the police questioned me like there was no tomorrow. Then when you came in, I thought to myself that it don't make no difference how hard you try to go straight, life don't let you."

"That was never my intent, Mr. Falls."

"Wes," he corrected.

"That was never my intent, Wes. I thought, though, that since you knew Burt, you might know what dangerous people he knew and what might have happened to him."

"I'll give you the skivvy on me and Burt. Then you can judge for yourself whether I can be of help. You got a minute? I don't want to keep you? I can call back?"

"I'm fine."

"There was a time," he said, "that Burt and me was like brothers. We was in juvy together, and then again when we went to do some hard time in Milan. He got out before I did so I looked him up when I got sprung. Hardly gave me the time of day—acted like my dropping in at his place was an insult. So I left, moved to Ohio, got day laborin' jobs for over a decade and pretty much forgot my old friend Burt. Then my luck started to change in a miracle-like way. I got a job back here, and shortly after that, I won the Michigan lottery, over a hundred thousand dollars. My picture was in the paper and everything. Well, a day or so after the article was in the paper, Burt shows up on my doorstep. A buddy of ours from prison had called him about my good luck. He said he was in bad trouble, that his little girl was dying, and he needed thirty thousand dollars for her surgery. You can say I'm dumb as dog shit— pardon my language—for doing it, but I gave him the money. I'd seen his little girl that day I dropped in, and she was a cute little thing. And we was good friends a long time ago. A man needs to remember his friendships. At first Burt was real good about paying it back. Two hundred a month. We'd set it up that way so he didn't have to feel broke making the payments. I'm the kind of person don't need much money so I was glad to loan it to him. We was friends again, and it felt good. Then about two years ago, the payments started bein' few and far between. A year ago they stopped coming period. I tried to get him on the phone, sent him a registered letter, too, but never heard back. The same friend who'd told Burt about my good luck called to talk and during our conversation told me that Burt had developed a bad gambling habit, was borrowing from everyone and getting in deep, deep shit—pardon me again, ma'am. So I finally figured out that his daughter was never sick. The only one in trouble was Burt and he probably used my money to keep square-headed guys from breaking every bone in his body."

"Did you confront him?'

"Tried to once, but his daughter was there, and I didn't want to scare her. In truth, it was my fault, too, for being so stupid. So Burt goes and gets himself killed, and I'm out most of thirty thousand dollars. I went to a lawyer to see if he could help me, but all he found out was that Burt was broke. So I was out another five hundred dollars for the lawyer whose only help was to tell me he couldn't help."

"So why did you get so angry at me when I asked about Burt?"

"Guess it brought back a lot of bad memories. I'm going to the Save Your Soul Community Church in Lawrence. I became a believer while I was in prison, and the preacher at Save Your Soul did some time there a long time ago. Him and me both believe in redemption. My faith has taught me to forgive and forget, so I thought I owed you an apology."

"You don't, but thanks. I probably owe you one."

"I know that God has forgiven me already. He made sure that I won another lottery. This one was even bigger than the last one. God forgives and forgets, too, I guess."

I believed Wes. I know there are ex-cons who have made a career of manipulating lies into the truth, but the way Wes handled the whole thing with me told me he wasn't one of them. I didn't know what put him in prison and didn't want to know. He was out now, and I'd bet my trust fund he wouldn't be going back. "Wes, I really appreciate your call and am happy for your good luck."

"Sure never saw myself as lucky, but the Savior has blessed me. It's funny because something told me to buy that second ticket. That's how carefully the Lord has looked after me. And Dottie, one of the women in my church, looks after me too. She don't even know I'm a rich man, but she loves me. We got something special and as soon as I can save some money that wasn't easy to come by, I'm going to get her a ring, a little diamond because Dottie doesn't like flashy things. I want to work for the ring I give her."

"Good for you."

As I was putting down the phone from talking to Wes, Aggie burst into my house waving a magazine and shouting, "She's done it!"

"You're going to scare Messy, Aggie. Who's done what?"

"That woman who had those ten babies through artificial intelligence or something, I forget what they call it. She just had four more, three are white and one is black. Did you even know that was possible?"

I could smell the whiskey. "How about we get some coffee and I show you what I've been working on." I walked her slowly to the kitchen. She headed for the whiskey cupboard but I wheeled her away and put her in a chair. "Sit. I'll make coffee."

"You think I'm lying," she flipped through the pages. "Here it is."

"I believe you. You're the one who taught me that truth is often stranger than fiction."

"It is. I love this new magazine, and you will too. It's called *The National Scoundrel*. Hilda gave me a subscription for my birthday."

"Aggie, did I miss your birthday!"

"Nope. You got me that spa package. My birthday was in August, but Hilda didn't have the money then."

I breathed a sigh of relief.

"And look what I brought us." She held up a small sack. "Two éclairs fresh from Hilda's kitchen."

"The best!" I reached into the sack.

"Oh, and it looks like Luke Barrett is the murderer, but you knew that, didn't you?"

"Luke? Luke Barrett? Where did you ever hear that?"

"My scanner."

Why do I bother asking.

"I guess Trey has some new evidence that he's been keeping quiet about."

"Aggie, who are you kidding? Trey couldn't keep a secret if his life depended on it. Luke's not the murderer. I'd bet all of Leland's money on it."

"That's a serious bet." She picked up a toothpick from the little canister I keep for her on the table. She dug away at something between her front teeth.

"Another name surfaced a little while ago," I told her. "I checked him out, but don't think he's the one we're looking for."

"Wes Falls," she continued to maneuver the toothpick.

"How did you know?" *Oops! Forgot again.*

"Scanner. I heard the police talking," she said matter-of-factly. "But his alibi checked out."

"And you know this because you heard it on the scanner?"

"No, I know people who go to his church, and one of them was at Hilda's when I picked up these éclairs."

"I met him today and just got off the phone from talking to him. He works for Charley."

"Isn't it a small world," she was a little sarcastic at Charley's name. "My second cousin, Harriet—the family calls her Dottie—has been going with Wes. The family wasn't too pleased about it because he has a shady past. Then we got to counting how many of us has done time, and it turns out we have no reason to be judging anyone. Dottie's helped him find Jesus Christ, and he's now been saved."

"Okay." Aggie and I have different views of the same God so I always get away from discussing religion as soon as possible. "Jenny Lundy is the one who brought up Wes's name. She said her dad and he had a bad argument and that Wes owed Burt a bunch of money."

"That little girl needs to believe the best of her father, but there's no way that anyone owed Burt money. He was into everyone in town. It's a good thing Elli died or he wouldn't have had a roof over his head. He'd lost his house. And at one time or another, everyone in this town has had an argument with Burt. He was a P-U-K-E."

"I'm desperate for information and Jenny was my last hope."

"You need a man to get your mind off murder, and Charley Cotter is not the man."

"Aggie, you have to cut him some slack. Even my mother has warmed to Charley. You and Scoop are the only holdouts."

"Scoop doesn't like him because Charley could be the son of Scoop. I don't like him because you have a sweet, tender heart, and a man like that will break it."

"He won't, Aggie. You'll see. So now I'm back to square one, and his name is Trey Davis."

Aggie's face registered her confusion. "What do you mean?"

"Jenny Lundy has been seeing Trey on the sly and has fallen under his slant-eyed, conniving spell. I saw her with him in Grand Rapids when I was there with my mother—when Trey was supposed to be dating Lacy!"

"Hilda and I saw them at Tasty Duck in Lawrence, too. They were tucked away in a dark corner and were pretty much all over each other. It was after he and Lacy were through, though, so I wasn't worried, except for poor Jenny."

If someone didn't find the murderer fast, Jenny Lundy might be the next unwitting victim. I felt I should warn her, but decided to wait until I gathered concrete evidence.

Thank God for Charley who helped me get Aggie into the guest bedroom. "Is it good for her to drink like this?" he asked as he gently slid her into bed.

"Are you going to be the one to stop her?" I asked.

"Not me. I have much more serious duties to attend to."

"Such as?"

"Such as taking care of my woman." He lifted me into his arms and carried me into my bedroom where he gently slid me into bed.

Chapter Sixteen

"You're the last person I expected to have show up here." Trey's narrow eyes narrowed even more, and I took a certain satisfaction in seeing that his muddy brown hair was thinning and graying, much to his chagrin, I imagined.

I knew no one would advise me to confront Trey, but I also knew taking other people's advice hadn't gotten anyone very far in solving the murders.

"Trey, I have a couple of questions to ask you." I pulled a chair up to his desk since he didn't invite me to sit.

"Don't get too comfortable, I have a lot going on," he shuffled the papers on his desk. "This job doesn't do itself."

Here goes. "More to the point, Trey, this job doesn't seem to get done. It's been weeks, and you've thrown out a lot of red herrings, but no one believes Luke Barrett killed anyone, and you can bet that Wes Falls didn't. In fact, they seem to have a lot less to hide than you do."

"Before you go any further, I want you to know who you're dealing with." He took my hand and squeezed it to the point of almost unbearable pain. "A lot of people in this town are grateful to me for what I've done for them. Very grateful."

"You must be talking about the people who've locked their keys in their cars. I hear you're extremely efficient at helping those people."

"And you're supposed to be a very smart girl. But you do dumb things. Driving at night alone. Rushing head first into toilets. People are saying that your Chicago boyfriend broke up with you, and you're nearly suicidal. We'd hate to lose you, Sam."

"What people?" I totally ignored his threat.

"I don't feel free to say, but you know how fast gossip travels here. Deadly fast." And there it was, the blood-chilling stare that convinced me Trey Davis was up to his ears in the murders and that also convinced me that he would love to see me as dead as the last murder victim.

"You're practically admitting that you've been involved in the murders."

"I'm admitting nothing," he leaned across the desk and into my face. "I'm saying that you better start appreciating what I do for you and others. And before you run screaming that you think you know something about me, just remember that your father is a drunk with heart trouble. He may not have long for this world."

Now it was my turn to lean. "You big, dumb creep! Maybe you've spent your life here, but I'm from Chicago, and you haven't seen anything until you see how Chicago treats people it wants to get rid of. Don't you dare threaten me or my father! What *you* should do is get a lawyer because you'll need one." I shoved the chair back and strode out the door. I hoped he didn't notice how rubbery my legs were, partly from white hot anger and partly from sheer terror. I knew I'd just stared into the face of pure evil.

"Charley is such a doll," Lacy said. "He's loaning me Jersey to see if he can't get the charges dismissed against Luke."

After my brief but highly-illuminating and death-defying conversation with Trey, I'd needed to steady myself, so I'd stopped in to Mabel's for my favorite sandwich.

"I thought you found Luke boring," I said watching her pour us glasses of iced tea. I was indescribably happy to be away from Trey and wondered how fabulous Lacy had ever let him dominate her for so long.

"I like Luke. He's a sweet guy. I'm just not attracted to him. And you and I both know that Luke is not the murderer."

Just that minute, a nervous-looking Luke walked in the door followed by a pretty rumpled-looking man. *He must be Jersey*, I thought, but he sure didn't look like any world-beating lawyer. Charley was the last to enter.

"I saw you leaving Trey's office," Charley said. "We'll talk about that later."

"I just stopped in to see Trey." On that, the fire in his eyes lessened.

"Take me along next time," he said sternly. "But for now, Sam and Lacy, I want you to meet one of my oldest and best friends—Malachi White, AKA, Jersey."

"It is so nice to meet you." Jersey had a firm, gentle handshake, "and you." When he smiled at Lacy, she actually blushed.

"I hate to cut this short," Charley said, "but we have a little business to conduct."

"Sure," Lacy and I said together as we watched the three become very hush-hush as a server I didn't recognize poured coffee and took their order.

"New guy?" I pointed to the server as Lacy and I walked away.

"I was going to fire Jenny, but she called in this morning and quit. I figure that this guy won't try to date the fellow I'm dating." She took another look at him. "At least I hope he doesn't."

Trey's threat took more out of me than I first thought so instead of going back to the paper, I went home. I opened the door of my house to an indescribably wonderful smell.

"Aunt Cathy's vegetable soup," I said to my mother who was stirring an enormous pot of soup. On the little kitchen TV, Aggie was watching *I am a Teenage Zombie.*

"We thought we'd make you soup and keep you company."

"And make sure I don't get my head stuck in a toilet again, right?"

"Kinda right," my mother smiled. "I just worry about your living alone here."

"Charley's here a lot," I reassured her.

"I worry about that too." She laughed. "I guess there's just no pleasing me."

"Your father is fit to be tied. I've never seen him so angry." She put some amaretto creamer in my coffee. "He called to say that Trey Davis had stormed into the paper and said you were harassing him. You didn't, did you?"

"If you call spending a few minutes with someone and telling him what you think of him, then I guess you could say I was harassing him."

"Oh, Sam." My mother wilted against the stove. "Unless your father forces you to, don't tell him what you just told me."

I wanted to tell her all about Trey. I wanted to tell everyone about my confrontation with him, but a small part of me was worried he'd do as he threatened and hurt the people I love. I had to know how to stop him before I told everyone what I knew about the monster in the police uniform.

"I know Scoop loves me, but he has a very odd way of showing it sometimes." I said.

"And you think this is news to me?" My mother stopped stirring and looked as if she was about to say more.

"I'll get it," I said when the doorbell rang. "Hello." I was surprised to see Jersey, still tousled, standing there.

"Charley had some work but gave me the directions to get here. Do you mind?"

My mother had joined me at the door and did a not-so-subtle double take when she saw Jersey. Even a bit messed up, he was a very good-looking guy. I introduced them and then led him into the living room because Aggie had fallen sound asleep in the TV room. "We can talk here."

"Good. Charley said you could fill me in a bit about Luke and his relationship with Trey Davis. Charley is sure that Trey has set Luke up."

"I would put nothing past Trey," I said.

"What makes you sure he can't be trusted?"

I told him what I knew, leaving out my last conversation with Trey.

"So no one knows where the money for the horse farm came from?" Jersey wrote fast as he asked questions rapid-fire. "I have some people who can look into that and get some answers."

I couldn't help noticing there was a huge dark spot on the beige tie Jersey loosened.

"Ketchup," he said. "I flew in from New York this morning, grabbed a car, and had every intention of showering at Charley's. My luggage, however, didn't arrive with me. And Charley is a good three inches taller so borrowing anything from him is out."

"I'd loan you something if I could," I laughed.

"Charley said you have a great sense of humor. He has *many* flattering things to say about you. I was eager to get here and see the girl who won Fast Charley's heart."

"Fast Charley?"

"Not what you think," he laughed. "Charley and I ran track at prep school. He always ran the last leg of the relay because of his speed."

"Sure. I bet that's what it was."

"Seriously. God, don't tell him I used his old nickname. He'll kill me. I will tell you that no one ever had a better friend than Charley. He's true blue. My dad lost his job when I was in 10th grade and my parents were going to have to pull me out of school. Suddenly, the school gave me a full ride. I was a senior before I realized that there was no such thing as a full-ride at that place. When I confronted Charley about it, he said that I was too good a roommate to lose so he'd told his dad about my having to leave school. From then on, Charley's dad paid for everything, including college and law school. My dad suffered a depression after he lost his job and never had a good job again. Charley and his dad are the reasons I'm here helping Luke Barrett. I know the value of pro bono."

"Look what she brought," my mother returned with Lacy and a tray of something great looking. Lacy, her long hair pulled back with gold wisps framing her face, had managed to change into a turquoise silk blouse and grey wool slacks. She was beyond beautiful.

"Lacy, isn't it?" Jersey rose and helped her set the platter of her specialty tiramisu on the table in front of the fireplace.

"I'd better be going," she slowly backed out.

"No! Stay!" I realized I'd come on too strong so I modulated my tone, "Jersey stopped to get some information on Trey. You're the expert on that subject."

Lacy's eyes begged me not to reveal the beating she'd taken at Trey's hands.

"We'd just started talking when you arrived," I quickly said to relieve her anxiety.

"Sit here." Jersey motioned to Lacy to sit next to him. According to Charley, Jersey was no player, but I knew Lacy well enough to know he was doing all the right things as far as she was concerned. "So how do you know Trey Davis?" he asked.

"We've dated on and off for the past few years. I'm embarrassed to say it aloud. We even lived together for a short time. He really isn't a very nice person, and I know a lot of girls say that about their exes, but even when I dated him, I knew he had a dark side. That's on me, I guess."

"If he didn't treat you well," Jersey's aquamarine eyes seemed to attach to Lacy's, "that's on him. Now, can you give me some specifics regarding him?"

"Women, there were other women all through the years that we dated," she said.

"He's crazy," I heard Jersey say sotto voce. "So," he spoke louder, "other than his problem with womanizing, did you ever know him to be violent?"

"He was always getting into bar fights, until he became a policeman. Then I think he used his uniform to get guys to back away. He's a bully. Everyone who ever knew him in school knew that. He was always picking on some poor weakling."

"Sounds like a charmer. Did you ever know him to be violent with women?"

"Is there a reason you're asking these questions?" Lacy's demeanor telegraphed that she thought he knew about her beating at Trey's hands.

"I am a little curious about the guy since I'm sure he's falsely accused Luke. There's no way that Luke Barrett sliced Mabel Pollock up." Jersey stopped because Lacy had become visibly agitated.

"Mabel was Lacy's aunt," I said.

"Oh, my gosh. I'm so sorry." He took one of her shaking hands in his and covered it with his remaining hand. "If Charley told me that, I've forgotten. I don't know when I've felt worse."

"I knew him to be violent. At least four times he knocked me into a wall or down the stairs. This last time was the worst and final time because he went for my face. I thought he was going to kill me." It spilled out of her as if she'd been desperate to release it.

"Lacy! Oh, Lace, why didn't you say something? I didn't know about the other times." I felt sick to my stomach.

"Because I thought I'd provoked him, that I'd driven him to it. And I know you, honey. You'd have marched into his office and gotten your beautiful face smashed in."

She didn't know how close she was to the truth. In his office not that long ago, Trey looked as if he would like to have punched me until my face looked like bread dough.

"Do either of you know," Jersey was angry, "what Trey might have against Luke?"

"Now let me think," Lacy smiled, "Luke's richer, better looking, smarter, and a hell of a lot more likeable than Trey."

"Did you and Luke date?"

"A couple of times. He's a good guy, but no spark."

"Spark's important." Jersey looked as though Lacy had already lit one in him. I hoped he wasn't too milquetoast for her because they looked great sitting side by side.

"I wonder if we should warn Jenny about Trey," I said. "Jenny Lundy is the daughter of one of the victims and the great niece of another one. She's sweet and innocent. Trey has been seen with her."

"I doubt that he's going to pull anything for a while," Lacy said. "He's starting to get the drift that we're onto him."

"How do you know that?" Jersey stopped writing.

"He absolutely hates Sam and her dad. He blames them for giving him a bad name all over town. He's told me that numerous times."

"You didn't tell me that," I said.

"I didn't want to hurt your feelings, and besides who cares what that putrid excuse for a human being thinks!"

"Lacy," Jersey smiled, "you have a great way of telling it just like it is. In my business, I get tired of people who game and manipulate the system."

"Trey would be the champion gamer and manipulator, but thanks for your compliment. I have to get back to work so I'd better scoot."

"How about you drop me off at Charley's? I walked here because Charley ordered a company car for me, and it won't be delivered until tomorrow."

"Have you eaten? I can take you with me, feed you some of Aunt Mabel's world-famous meat loaf, and take you to Charley's as soon as my replacement arrives."

"That's very hospitable of you."

"You're a good guy. You deserve a good meal." She seemed startled as Jersey helped her put her leather coat on and opened the door for her.

It's time, I thought, *that she dates someone who treats her like she should be treated, like Charley treats me.*

"It was nice to meet you, Mr. Jersey," my mother said as the rest of us laughed.

"It's been a pleasure meeting you," he said mostly to my mother. "Thanks for letting me barge in. And thanks for filling me in on some things I didn't know." The last part he said mostly to me.

My mother left shortly after Jersey. Charley arrived right after I'd showered, slipped into a pair of flannel PJs and poured myself a glass of wine.

"I'm a heat-seeking missile," he buried his face in my neck as soon as I set down the wine. "Jersey called me to say that you are every bit the knockout I'd told him you are."

"That's very kind, but I'm here to tell you that I was not the knockout he spent his time staring at."

"Your mother?" he laughed. "Are you telling me that Jersey was hitting on your mother?"

"No. He couldn't take his eyes off Lacy. I think the feeling is mutual."

"That's great for him. He had a bad break up a couple of years ago, and I don't think he's been serious since. I'm not sure that he's Lacy's kind, though. She always falls for those bad boys."

"I know. Luke Barrett held no interest for her."

"And that's another reason I'm here. Jersey called to say he had a message on his phone from Luke. All charges have been dropped. I don't think there was ever much of a case, but I'm glad that Jersey could help Luke. He won't be doing much criminal work at The Foundation so I think he was glad to flex his defense attorney muscles one last time."

"You said that telling me about Luke was the other reason you're here. What's the first reason?"

"This, baby, this." He kissed me. "Hmmm, do I detect raspberry something?" He talked and kissed at the same time.

"Tiramisu," I put my arms around him, and leaned my head back so he could kiss every inch of my neck.

"This may not be the time to ask, but is there any left?"

"Yes," I pretended to angrily push him away and went to refrigerator to retrieve some of Lacy's dessert.

"Should I be upset that I'm playing second fiddle to dessert?"

"You're my fantasy—have been ever since that night on the lake. Even when I first met you, I could tell you were always going to be your own fascinating person. I admired that even though I was pretty much a party-loving jerk. Not you, though. That night when people got stupid drunk, you left and went for a swim."

"And nearly died." I gently stroked his cheek and then planted kisses on it. "I don't think I ever thanked you for that. You were frantic that I was dying, but all I could think of was that Charley Cotter's lips were on mine."

"And would have stayed there a lot longer if there hadn't been a crowd watching what they were sure was your imminent demise."

"Then the policemen, firemen, and my parents were all there at once. Scoop was screaming at you and threatening to throw you in jail. My mother and Leland had chartered a plane from Chicago and were horrified I was with you, that I'd actually slipped out of my room to be with a crowd of half drunk kids."

"Lacy's boyfriend was the one who concocted the big idea for you and Lacy to slip out of your houses, as I remember. Has she ever had a good boyfriend?" he laughed.

"Now about that thank-you," I pulled him on top of me and wrapped my legs around him. "Mr. Cotter, you were such a gentleman that night, and I appreciate it more than you know, but you no longer have to be a gentleman."

"That's a relief, Ms. Hayes, because I'm far too hungry and not for tiramisu. How about I slip into something more comfortable?"

Chapter Seventeen

"I think Trey is the mastermind of the misery we've all been experiencing, but I have to catch him red-handed."

"Careful." Charley rested his hand gently of the back of my neck. It was the week before Christmas and we were watching *The Wire* reruns with Lacy and Jersey. Jersey had brought lobster to cook for us, and Lacy had brought salads and dessert. My mother called to say she and Scoop were going to a movie. All would have been right with the world if the world weren't crumbling right beneath our feet. I'd had two more cryptic, but undeniably threatening, emails and the person I should have been able to report them to was probably the one who was sending them.

"I'm out of ideas," I said loudly enough that Jersey and Lacy, who'd been pretty much wrapped around each other, sat up straight. "We need help and no one is giving it. The state police can't find certain deeds and records, and Trey struts around as though he's untouchable."

"Maybe it's time for my father's detective agency. What do you think, Jersey?"

"Your father owns a detective agency?" Charley continually surprised me.

"He doesn't own it, but for years, he's used one from time to time to verify employee records and make sure things at The Foundation and at Cotter Manufacturing are on the up and up. I wasn't aware of it until after he died and his accountant showed me an enormous bill from The Spinazze Agency in New York City. I called to see what was going on, and one of the partners filled me in."

"Why did he use one so far away?" I couldn't envision anything in Cotter's Corner that would demand a big city detective operation. "It seems like it would have been easier to go through a head hunter or employment agency. New York? It's as if your father wanted to keep the whole thing quiet."

"You won't believe this, but I actually know that agency," said Lacy. "My Aunt Mabel had a couple of bills from them, too. Every time I went to ask her about them, she pulled them out of my hand and said her business with them was done."

"That is weird." Charley said.

"It's not so crazy," I said. "They were both business people and had to check the histories of people they hired. In your aunt's case," I looked at Lacy, "she might have wanted to check on her renters' backgrounds, too."

"Maybe. But I'm not sure that I think that was the reason. At the time," Lacy said, "I thought, 'Who am I to question Aunt Mabel?' More and more, I wish I had."

When Lacy and Jersey had left, Charley and I put the dishes in the dishwasher. "I think we've been matchmakers."

"Yep. And now it's just us, peaches, and I'm very happy to be alone with you." He stood behind me as I rinsed off a few of the dishes.

I didn't dare tell Charley that as sexy as he was and as much as I wanted to jump his hot body, I couldn't get my mind off the evening's conversation.

"Don't you think it's strange that both your dad and Lacy's aunt used the same agency?"

"Hey!" Charley stopped burning kisses into the back of my neck. "Here I am giving you my very best seduction routine, and all I get is talk about the detective agency."

I pulled his delicious face toward mine and kissed those oh-so-tempting lips. "Sorry. You know I'd love to do this forever, but we might be saving another life here."

"Since you put it that way, I'll forgive you tonight."

"I so appreciate that. The last thing I want to say on the subject is that I'd love you to go on a little fishing expedition tomorrow. Please call the agency and see if there was a connection between your father and Mabel Pollock."

"I can see that there's only one way I'm going to have you totally to myself. It has to be forty thousand feet up."

"What?"

"I'm not going to call the Spinazze brothers to ask questions. I'm going there. You know New York City is wonderful this close to Christmas. Come with me and pick out your present."

"Are you serious?"

"I have a pretty clear calendar tomorrow so tell Scoop that I'll have the jet fired up and ready to go as soon as you grab some work you can take with you on the plane."

"You're really taking me to New York?"

"It's the only way I can keep you away from toilets, head bangers, and ringing doorbells. I'm a desperate man and this calls for desperate measures."

"Let's go upstairs and I'll see if I can't relieve a little of that desperation. How about it?"

"I thought you'd never ask."

The next day was surreal. We had champagne before we took off and orgasms before we landed. The plane looked Presidential, and the crew had obviously been with Charley in similar situations.

"They look like they've been taught to 'hear no evil, see no evil, and speak no evil.' Exactly how many girls and women have you brought to your own personal mile high club?"

"Sam, you know I've been far from a saint. I think the better question is how many more will there be? None."

"Such a perfect answer." I pressed my body into his. I had no intention of getting any work done.

Usually I'm very relieved when planes land. Not this time. Being that high up with Charley was as close to heaven as I might ever get.

And The Spinazze Detective Agency might be excellent, but it certainly didn't look it. First, the part of town it was in was a little scary, about as far from Park Avenue as possible. Once we survived the frightening, bumpy elevator ride to the seventh floor, we saw a set of offices straight out of a 1950's B-movie. Scoop's venerated Mike Hammer would be right at home in the Spinazze brothers' agency.

Even the secretary, a woman a little too made up with badly dyed orange-blonde hair, was straight out of central casting. Busty and bawdy, I imagined she'd slept with pretty much everyone in the agency—male or female. The office reeked of smoke, though there were "No Smoking" signs posted on every wall.

"Can I help you?" The woman's face showed signs of wear. She was older than I'd first thought.

"We're here to see Randy Spinazze." Charley handed her his card. She took a second to let go of his hand.

"Let me see if he's ready for you." Her plump hind-end became a metronome as she slowly walked away.

"*She's* definitely ready for you," I kidded Charley while the woman was in the other office.

"No one rides in the plane but you, baby," he said *á la* Humphrey Bogart. It was hot.

"He'll see you now." Miss Bawdy Blonde was awkwardly formal as she admitted us to the inner sanctum.

"Mr. Cotter?" The man who introduced himself as Spinazze stood and shook our hands. His hand was warm and moist. Yuck.

"This is my friend, Samuels."

I was glad Charley hadn't given my whole name because the best word I could think of to describe Randy Spinazze was seedy, even his clothes had that Rico Suave tinge to them. "I'm glad to meet you, Miss Samuels."

"Her name is Samuels." Charley had noticed Spinazze's leering at me, and his tone said he didn't like it. "Her first name is Samuels."

"Oh, I'm sorry." Both his attitude and tone became more respectful.

"I would have called, but I want this conversation kept in strictest confidence," Charley said after we sat down on leather chairs that were at most ten percent cheap leather and the rest plastic.

"Of course," the agency's owner said. "My grandfather started this agency, and we've had a robust business ever since. If we had been indiscreet, we wouldn't still be around."

"I'm sure that's the case, but I felt I needed to reiterate the importance of discretion," Charley smiled his oh-so-charming smile.

"Rest assured that what's said in this office stays in this office."

"My father used you for various investigations that I wasn't privy to before his death. I've recently learned that a friend's aunt also has used your agency. I'm hoping you'll be able to fill in some blanks for me."

Spinazze fidgeted with a paperclip and then said, "You know that client information is private. Just as you want me to keep why you're here a secret, other clients are equally eager to protect their privacy. I would help you if I could, but that would be the grossest assault on confidentiality."

"Two of your ex-clients have recently met untimely deaths." Charley wasn't angry but he was, let's say, extremely firm. "One of them was my father. The other is the woman I just referred to who also used your agency. Her name was Mabel Pollock, and she was murdered. We need your help."

"If I reveal something to help you, then others will find out, and pretty soon my two brothers and I will be *persona non grata* in this business. We have wives, ex-wives, children, and stepchildren who depend on this agency, to say nothing of the ditz in the front office who is my cousin. I'm worn out from keeping the angry wives of her boyfriends away from her throat."

"I promise that the source of what you tell me will never be divulged. I also promise you that if you give us some valuable information, I'll throw enough business your way to put all those kids and step kids through the best schools and colleges in this area." Charley leaned across the desk toward Randy, whose body language signaled he loved the tit for tat suggestion. Charley definitely had his attention.

"Maybe we can work this out so you get what you need without my totally blabbing."

"Tell me how," Charley said. "Can you tell me if my dad and Mabel used you for the same issues sometimes?"

"No, I can't flat out answer that. It's too close to being unethical. Not that I haven't walked that fine line between honor and a dollar." His laugh insinuated that Randy Spinazze had known his share of dirty deals. "It would be better if you could give me some categories and ask which of the categories your dad and this Mabel were likely to have needed help in."

"Okay. First, did they both come to you at the same time?" Charley could have been a lawyer.

"Same need, not same time."

"Thanks. Now we're getting somewhere." Charley loosened his tie.

"Is there a chance that each wasn't aware that the other was using your agency?"

"Yes, but I doubt it." Randy played with the pack of cigarettes in his left shirt pocket.

"Let's try to get closer to the reason they came to see you," Charley rolled the paperclip around on the desk as he spoke. "Did they seem to be worried that someone was going to hurt them?"

"How do you mean *hurt*?" Randy asked.

"You're giving us a clue, aren't you?" I asked. "Did they think someone was following them, stealing from them, or blackmailing them?"

"The last one. That's all I'm saying." He stood, signaling that our interview was over.

On our way out the door, I stopped and turned. "Can you tell us one more thing? How long ago did all this take place?"

"I've given you enough." Randy wiped his sweaty hands on his pants. Then he shook Charley's hand. "I'll look forward to hearing from you soon. Quid pro quo, bro."

The outer office was empty. "I'm not sure we got anything," Charley said. "But I do think that my dad used the agency to check a lot more than references."

I nodded. We left the office and found the secretary smoking on the stairwell.

"How long have you worked here?" I asked her.

"Long enough." She took a puff. "You're asking about your dad, aren't you?" She studied Charley. "I knew him, very well."

It was a statement Charley seemed to dread addressing. "So how did you know my dad?"

"Oh," she laughed, "I didn't *know* him know him like you're thinking. I felt sorry for him. Over the past few years he'd come here once in a while to do his business, but he seemed so lonely. So we got to having lunch, that's all—just lunch. He paid. I listened. He talked about you, how he didn't think he was a good father to you. And he told me about your mother. Mostly he told me he was worried that his world could come crashing down. He drank a little too much at those lunches so he probably talked more than he might have otherwise."

"Did he tell you why he thought his world was about to end?" I asked.

"No, but I think it had something to do with that Mabel's business too. Sometimes they'd meet as one was going and the other coming. They didn't seem to be that close, and he never brought her to lunch with us. I waited out here to tell you that your father was a good man. Once I needed hernia surgery, and he paid for it. We never did nothing but talk, and when we were done, he always slipped me a little something. I know a lot of guys, but he's the only one who wanted me to listen. That's all he ever asked."

"I really appreciate your taking the time to tell me this," Charley said. When he shook her hand I noticed he slipped her several twenty dollar bills. "From my father," he said. "Good luck."

"I am so glad to be leaving this city." Charley was pouring us both stiff drinks as we prepared for take off. "That was sad, wasn't it? I mean that picture of my dad just wanting someone to listen. Oh, my gosh, I forgot to pick up something for you for Christmas."

"Oh, Charley, that's fine."

"Here." He reached into his topcoat and pulled out a long, unmistakable blue box. "I'll have more at Christmas but I wanted you to have this."

When I opened the box there was the most beautiful and intricate gold charm bracelet I'd ever seen. The charms were dotted with diamonds, pearls, rubies, and other precious gems. A golden retriever had emerald eyes. A heart was surrounded by diamonds. A typewriter had onyx keys, and other equally meaningful charms held equally expensive jewels. "I've never seen anything this wonderful. Charley, when did you do this?"

"Over a month ago, shortly after our first meeting. I started thinking about the years I've known you and what I knew about you. Then I passed Tiffany's and saw a similar bracelet. You like it?"

"I love it. And I love you."

"You know I love you. Sam, I think I've loved you forever."

My tears came unbidden. I tried not to blink so they wouldn't stream down my face. "I'm so glad."

"I'm ready to give you a ring, but I know you. You'll think it's too quick. Still, you need to know it's on my mind. I'm a very focused, goal-oriented guy."

"Oh you are, are you?" As I put on the bracelet, Charley began kissing my wrist and worked his way up. I got no work done on the trip back either.

We both slept briefly after my mile-high thank you, but as we were getting ready to land, I said, "You know this may sound strange, but I think Lacy is somehow connected to the blackmail. I don't mean she was involved, but her father's prison release information was in Elli's mysterious envelope. It must mean something, or Elli wouldn't have asked Aggie to keep it hidden. And Lacy's aunt went to The Spinazze Agency with your father a couple of times. I don't know why, but I think today has been significant. We might be closer to the murderer that we think."

"You sound so knowledgeable, Ms. Hayes. It's a total turn on." As we landed, Charley's libido took off. "Down, boy. We're going to hit tarmac pretty soon. I have every intention of being fully dressed when we deplane."

"He's there." Charley waved at the policeman as we pulled into my driveway. "I look forward to a day when it's no longer necessary to have someone parked out front to protect your life."

"Me, too." I opened my front door and was mobbed by Messy. "You missed me?"

Charley ordered take out pizza, which we ate in front of my fire.

"Have you been able to process what Randy Spinazze said?" I asked.

"Not really. He was a pretty strange character, wasn't he?" Charley smiled. "I don't know what I expected, but if I was to paint a picture of a sleazy private eye, he would have come close."

"I know. I think he takes his work seriously, though."

"And I bet he's been into some very dangerous shit. People don't like their lives being investigated."

The phone rang next to Charley so he picked it up. After a few hard-to-discern words, he hung up. "That was your father. We need to go to plan B."

"What?" Wine and pizza had definitely clouded my thinking.

"Your mother and Scoop were eating at Mabel's when they noticed a lot of activity across the street at the jail—police cars, ambulances, and so forth."

"What happened?"

"That's what your dad went across the street to find out. Turns out that Trey Davis was murdered a couple of hours ago. The deputy is issuing a warrant for Luke. He's convinced that Luke got out of jail and killed the man who arrested him."

I could feel my throat tightening. I'd been wrong about about Luke. I must have been wrong about Trey, too.

Chapter Eighteen

Sheer panic is not like the jitters you get during a scary movie or the anxiety you feel before a big test. It's a sick-to-your-stomach, lightheaded feeling, and it's a thousand times worse than any fear you can imagine. That's how I felt the next day. When I wasn't jumping at every strange movement or noise, I was sitting with nervous-wreck Lacy. Her aunt and ex-boyfriend were dead, and a friend of hers had been arrested for murder. Her current love interest, Jersey, was spending every minute trying to keep Luke Barrett from spending the rest of his life in prison. I wasn't sure he didn't deserve to.

And if Luke wasn't the murderer, who was? I'd pinned all my suspicions on Trey. It had to be someone from town because the murders happened in Cotter's Corner, and the FBI had just joined the investigation because Snoop had called a friend who called a friend. Their investigators were convinced that the murderer knew some of the victims. And even worse, they were sure he was nearby.

Aggie was no help. She'd mobilized her slow-but-sure neighborhood watch group to help protect the town. "Hilda and me are the captains," she said. "We've got people all over town watching for the slightest sign of trouble. Then we'll attack!" She was serious. She was delusional.

Half of Aggie's walking wounded couldn't hold their eyes entirely open. And if their eyes were wide open, their vision was so impaired that they'd be little help. If I hadn't been so mad and so scared, I would have teased her. However, at the moment, anyone on guard for the murderer was a friend of mine.

"Overdose," was the first thing Charley said when he walked into the paper.

"What did you say?" I'd been trying to straighten out Scoop's version of the classifieds.

"They're saying Trey died from an overdose."

"Suicide?"

"No. Definitely murder. A chemo drug, an old one, was injected in a lethal dose."

"Every murder has been a little different. This one is the least violent but the most bizarre."

"This is no surprise to us." Charley sat on the side of my desk, "but the FBI feels we are dealing with a total psychopath."

"I've been thinking a little more about blackmail where your father is concerned. Do you have any idea of something that could have been used against him?" I'd put off bringing it up because Charley had unfinished, unresolved issues where his father was concerned.

"I've thought about that too. I'd like to say that my dad was an open book, but he wasn't. He was all secrets and contradictions. I'm telling only you this. After my mother was hospitalized, when I was too little to be much company for my father, he totally shut down. He had to be put in a private psychiatric hospital. They say he was a completely different man when he returned home. There were lots of women after that. I know this because I heard the staff talking over the years, and would see them rolling their eyes when they talked about him. I got mad at them for it, but I was also mad at my dad for chasing women while my mother was suffering in the hospital. I'm thinking someone got hold of the information and used it against him."

"But Mabel? Why would she be blackmailed? And why did they go to the same detective agency?"

"So you two are thinking," Scoop flew through the door, "what I've been thinking."

"What do you think we're thinking?" I asked.

"Blackmail. I heard you talking about it just now. Truthfully, it's been in my mind ever since your dad died, Charley, but I didn't know if you were grownup enough to hear what I know."

"And you know what?" Charley looked Scoop straight in the eyes.

"I know that your dad had a lot of problems and those problems bred a lot of trouble. Some of the trouble was with all ages and types of women. One of those women might have had a very dark story to tell."

"Scoop!" My dad had gone too far.

"It's okay, honey." Charley put his hand on my shoulder. "It's not the first time I've thought exactly the same thing. Tell me what you know, Scoop."

"I know a couple of things, and I've been quiet because your dad was pretty good to me. When I was drinking the hardest and at risk of losing everything, he made me a loan. I eventually paid it back, but he never made an issue of it. He let me pay as I could. I was pretty lost after Cat left me, and your dad said he knew what it was like to lose the woman you loved."

"He must have meant my mother," Charley said.

"That would have made this easier. The problem is that your mother was still alive." Scoop took a breath. "It was then I knew there was someone else in his life."

"You were lost after mother left you?" It was a new version of the old story.

"Let's stick to one subject at a time," Scoop lowered his eyes. "We'll get to that later, okay?"

I nodded.

"Women always made themselves available to your dad, Charley. He was good looking and rich, but up to the time your mother was hurt, your father was known to be totally faithful. That changed once he started blaming himself for what happened to her. It was part of his path to self destruction. So way before your mother died, I knew there was someone else who'd captured him body and soul. He was smiling again and had an almost light-heartedness about him. The rumor was that she was younger, and that he was totally in love with her. Most people let it drop there, but I knew that a beautiful young woman worked at the factory and that she, too, seemed to have found recent happiness. No longer did she look sad and stressed. She had an on again, off again boyfriend who was a town troublemaker, but he seemed a fleeting thing."

"You're talking about Lacy's mother, aren't you?" I was gob-smacked.

"Lacy's mother and my father?" Charley, too, was caught off guard.

"That's what I think. And here's the tough part to hear, Charley. I also think that the woman found out she was pregnant, but didn't tell the love of her life because he was married."

"Lacy is my father's daughter?" Charley was wide-eyed. "Lacy is my sister?"

"I think so. I have no concrete proof, but there's a lot of circumstantial evidence. Lacy's mother, Sheila, was determined to keep Robert Pickett thinking that the baby was his. And for a while it worked. Sheila was a good woman who would have worried that her husband might have killed Charles, Senior, if he'd known the truth. And in protecting your father, Charley, she put herself at risk and was killed by a man she should never have married."

"There's the link," Charley said. "My father and Mabel were struggling to keep Lacy from learning the truth. Someone else knew it and was blackmailing them."

"I think that's part of our puzzle. It doesn't explain Elli or Burt, but it's a plausible, partial solution."

"So Mabel knew about Lacy's father from the start?"

"I doubt that she knew from the start, but she was a smart old bird. I bet she figured it out early on. I had the FBI give me your father's old phone records. When Lacy was about three, Mabel started making calls to you father. And there were times recorded by the police that people heard them arguing so loudly that neighbors had called. My guess that after your mother died, Charley, Mabel told him that Lacy was his. By that time, the damage had been done, and his reputation would have been ruined if he'd publicly acknowledged Lacy. So he did the next best thing, he started giving Mabel buckets of money for Lacy. Remember the old story that Mabel's husband's accident insurance bankrolled the start of her business success? I spent the last couple of days going through records that my buddy at the FBI got me. The railroad gave Lacy's aunt five thousand dollars, hardly the hundreds of thousands Mabel claimed she received. Records show that it was Charley's dad who bankrolled Mabel's rise to business stardom."

"Did Lacy's dad ever learn who the father was?"

"I'm sure he didn't. Charley's dad would have died much sooner if he had."

"I still can't get over the fact that Lacy may be, probably is, my sister." Charley said.

"How do you feel about it?" I asked.

"Surprisingly good. I've always felt a connection to her, and this explains it. But Jersey had better watch himself. I intend to be a very protective older brother."

"How long have you thought this?" I turned to Scoop.

"Not long. Those FBI records opened other doors. And I was sure that at the root of all this was Trey Davis. He fits in perfectly as someone who grew up here, might have heard some of the gossip, and would be eager to capitalize on it. It would also explain how he got the money for the Trainor place. But with his death, we're back at square one."

"Not really. We know a lot and need to know more," I said. "We have to find a way to flush out the murderer. And we have to consider the possibility that there's more than one, terrifying as that prospect may be."

"Do you think we should tell Lacy what we know?" I asked.

"Wait. That girl's been through a lot. I think we're right about the conclusions we're drawing, but I think we need to be nearly one hundred percent sure."

"That would take a DNA test," Charley said.

"It may come to that," Scoop agreed.

"Now, where do we go next?" Charley asked.

I didn't need to answer it because Jersey came in. "Well, for the second time, we have sprung Luke. He had an air right alibi."

"Great." I hoped it was.

"Who's that?" Jersey looked out the window as Jenny walked by.

"Do you want an introduction?" I hoped he wasn't already looking for a Lacy replacement. "It's Burt Lundy's niece, Jenny."

"Jenny Lundy," he repeated. "I've heard that name a lot in these past two days, and do you ever notice that wherever she goes, murder seems to follow her?"

"What?" I said. "You're not saying that Jenny Lundy—that darling girl who is barely out of her teens—has anything to do with murder?'

"I'm not saying anything," Jersey smiled. "But she is very close to the victims when they pass from this world."

"And now you see why we call him Jersey," Charley laughed. "He's always looking for an angle. *The Sopranos* and *Boardwalk Empire*, you know." Charley gave Jersey a whack on the back.

They left me to finish the latté they'd brought me and to rethink what Jersey had just said. Had Jenny been used by the murderer to accomplish what he wanted? Sometimes things are so close to you that you don't see them. What Jersey had hinted at sounded preposterous at first, but as I considered how vulnerable Jenny was, I could see her falling in with bad company. And that could change her.

I went back to the paper. *Snooping* was not a column I'd been proud of lately. I promised myself I would pay more attention to it. I made sure the Christmas-sale ads were ready to go in the paper and also posted the winners of the recipe contest. Feeling bad about the way I'd thought about Annette Stancati lately, I heralded her asiago cheese bread recipe which was a first place winner in baked goods. I then edited a piece that the Cotter's Corner choir director had submitted about their upcoming production of *Fiddler on the Roof*. I wrote a note to myself to interview two of the principal players for the next edition. But nothing I wrote seemed important. What I wanted to write I couldn't:

We thought our town was safe, that we were impervious to anything bad happening here, but the events of the past few weeks have taught us differently. We walk down the same tree-lined streets we've always

*walked, but there's a difference. Some of our best
known and most-loved citizens are no longer walking
with us. They were victims of brutal crimes committed
by someone without a heart, without a soul. Come out
of the darkness, you bastard. Let us do to you what
you've done to so many others.*

It wasn't literary, and I could never print it, but I felt
so much freer having written it. In a way, the murderer
had taken all our lives, owned them, and changed them.
We were no longer able to experience the total freedom
we'd taken for granted. I'd never been depressed, not in
a serious way, but I knew at that moment, I was close.
And I was full of blinding rage that there might be
another murder I would be powerless to stop.

"Scoop is taking me for hotdogs at The Root Beer
Barrel. Would you like to meet us there?" My mother's
message sent an hour or so before, was on the machine
when I got home from work and from running a couple
of errands. My refrigerator was still stocked and though
a hot dog is so good once in a while, not tonight.

I ran Messy up and down the block ten times, not
easy with a snowy sidewalk. I should say I walked fast,
keeping Messy from pulling ahead and causing me to
fall. Then I fed both of us. I had some more of my
mother's turkey vegetable soup and a Lacy lemon bar.
Messy ate her dog food, grudgingly, once she caught
sight of the lemon bar.

Then I called Aggie, hoping to catch her before she
and Hilda headed for their every-other-night Bingo
game. We were done sewing quilt pieces until after the
holidays.

"Hey, Snoopy, I was just on my way out the door.
You're not home alone, are you?"

"Just for a few minutes, and you know that my
friendly policeman will be parked out front for the night
very soon." It was a lie, because the department called

and asked if it was all right to let them put the officer at the desk. Trey's death had left them short-handed. I was almost glad to be on my own, a big girl again.

"Can I call you when I get home from Bingo? Hilda's waiting."

"I'll make it quick. Tell me about Jenny Lundy. I was talking to someone a while ago, and something he said got me to thinking. Jenny has been closely connected to several of the victims. Do you think the murderer somehow involved her in his dirty work?"

"I think I've told you pretty much what I know about Jenny. She was the most beautiful little girl you ever saw, but we didn't see her much. That Burt kept a tight rein. When she went to live with the preacher and his wife, we saw her a little more, I guess. She was still beautiful, but the light in her eyes was gone. I guess the whole town feels a little guilty about not doing more to help her. I know she was a good student. I'd see her name on the honor roll a lot. Elli worried about her. Men were always asking her out, even before she was old enough to date. The men were questionable, too. Sometimes they were married. It wasn't a good situation as far as Elli was concerned. I think Elli thought Jenny might end up with a bum, like Burt. And she always worried about what he might be up to with her—you know—dirty old man kind of stuff."

"Do you think she could be easily talked into a scheme? Maybe she was coerced to pass on information or something."

"Trey used everyone," Aggie said, "and I'm sure Jenny was no exception. In what way do you think somebody used her?"

"Trey or someone else might have had her listen into conversations while she was working at Mabel's. He was such a dirt bag that he might have asked her to listen in on phone calls or read Mabel's mail. She might have found out who Lacy's real father was."

"Not surprised. A few of us noticed that when Lacy's dad was in prison, Sheila brightened and started taking care of her herself. She was a very pretty woman. Word was that she'd met someone while she worked at the factory."

"Aggie, I'm going to tell you something that you must not repeat. Lacy doesn't know anything about this, and we're not going to tell her yet." I then related what Scoop, Charley, and I surmised was the truth about Lacy's parentage.

"Wow! That makes sense. I knew there must be someone else, but I never once considered Charles Cotter. Now that I think about it, it's not an altogether crazy idea. And I do remember seeing that big limo of his cruising our streets once in a while. Sheila and Lacy lived in the next block over, you know. I never put two and two together. I'm slipping."

"We're all slipping. There were clues that we totally missed."

"Come to think of it, about the time that Sheila was murdered, Mr. Cotter went to a very dark place. He was drinking, swearing in public, and not caring what kind of women he was seen with. He got better, but it took a while. Then his wife died, and I think he went on living, but it was a living death, and miserable for Charley. I'm going to call Hilda and tell her to go on without me. I'll stop at your house on the way to Bingo. I thought of something that I don't want to say over the phone."

I didn't want to think how fast Aggie drove because she was at my door in no more than ten minutes.

"Where's the policeman?" she snapped as I helped her out of her plaid lumber jacket.

"Reassigned. I didn't want to tell you because I knew you'd blow a gasket. Charley's sleeping here nights, so I'm fine. "Now what's so important that you're going to be late for Bingo?"

"There's someplace else where Jenny might have picked up information. She worked at Cotter Manufacturing when she was a senior in high school. She was an intern, and it was a plum job. She bragged about it and worked there for at least a year. Burt made her quit when he got out of jail because he always insisted that he'd been unfairly fired from there. You tell me how it was unfair if all the money he'd stolen was found in his wallet, most of it anyway."

"Why couldn't you tell me this over the phone?"

"Who knows who's listening?" Aggie put her jacket back on. "This is all driving me to distraction. I intend to drink a lot. Hilda will probably have to drive me home."

"She can't see!" I shouted as Aggie closed the door. Now I had one more thing to worry about.

Chapter Nineteen

Jersey's new BMW was pretty much parked where I thought it would be: in front of Lacy's. I didn't want to interrupt anything, but I did want to share with Jersey that Jenny Lundy had worked at Cotter Manufacturing. I had no idea if or in what way Jenny might be connected, but Trey was clever and perhaps she was into something before she realized it. Then somehow the deal backfired and Trey was murdered. If that was true, Jenny would be a target.

"I was getting ready to call you." Jersey stood as I entered, and Lacy handed me a cup of warm coffee before I even got my coat off. "Charley got a call to go back to the shop and his cell was close to dying, so he told me to tell you that he'll be a few hours. I was getting ready to give you a call. He won't be happy that you're out and about alone."

"Just what *are* you doing out alone?" Lacy asked. "I thought the deal was that you'd stay home after dark as long as there's no policeman."

"I'm going home right after this," I said. "I thought about trying to see Jenny, but Mrs. Abbott probably would frown on my dropping in at this hour."

"Probably," Lacy laughed. "But she's not at the boarding house. She had to give her notice since she's leaving town, so she's staying at Elli's until she moves."

"Yeah, about that move. Costa Rica? I don't get that. I doubt she's ever been out of the state of Michigan. Maybe it was a plan that Trey had, and Jenny has decided to go ahead with it."

"I don't think so. Remember Trey bought the farm. I think he intended to stay there and be a gentleman farmer." Lacy warmed Jersey's coffee.

"Sorry," I said to him. "Some of this must still be gibberish. Lacy can fill you in on anything you don't already know about Jenny."

"Oddly, Jersey seems to know Jenny the best. We were so close to the situation that we totally overlooked the fact that she might be involved in some way." Lacy gave him a hug, which he didn't seem to mind.

"That's true," I laughed. "We needed you to arrive here a lot sooner," I said to Jersey.

"A lot sooner." Lacy gave Jersey what can only be described as the clichéd "knowing wink."

"I never figured out," I thought aloud, "how a girl who couldn't afford community college could afford Costa Rica."

"Oh, that I can answer," Lacy said. "Aunt Mabel left her fifty thousand dollars. She always felt sorry for Jenny."

"That's a lot of money for a girl like Jenny. I wonder if it's enough to kill for." Jersey looked at both of us.

Lacy and I started to say something but for the first time in a long time, we kept quiet.

I left Lacy's with more questions than I had when I arrived. So what had seemed a very bad idea a few minutes before now seemed like the only choice I had. I turned my car toward Elli's house, the one that Jenny Lundy now occupied, albeit temporarily.

It was spookily dark out, but my curiosity drove me to Jenny's temporary residence, where I hoped I would finally get some answers. The one bright spot was I didn't have to see May Abbott's dour demeanor again. Christmas was days away, and my only wish was to have the damn murders solved and to be able to enjoy life with Charley, not that I couldn't enjoy him despite what was going on in the external world. Still, Charley, hot chocolate, and chestnuts roasting over an open fire were so much better than murder and mayhem.

My first surprise was the shiny silver Prius parked in Elli's driveway. Jenny either had company or a new car.

"I hope it's not too late," I said as Jenny, this time fully dressed in a Michigan sweatshirt and skinny jeans that hugged her enviable figure, greeted me in the doorway. She was definitely a man-magnet, whether she wanted to be or not.

"You know, Sam, it's not a very good time. I have a lot of packing to do and tasks to complete."

"Just a few minutes? I wanted to tell you personally how sorry I was to hear about Trey." I watched for a reaction, but no visible signs of sorrow appeared.

"I do feel bad that he's dead," she said. "You know, he actually left me some money, can you believe that? He had these plans that we were going to live together, but I told him I was too young to be tied down. He started to hit me, but I told him I'd report him. Then he told me he was going to change his will. Aren't I lucky he didn't have time!"

"Lucky," I said.

"It was the age thing, you know," she wiped some pretty unconvincing tears from her eyes. I was getting a whole new picture of Jenny. "He's not really my type." Jenny was a pretty cool kiddo. Suddenly she seemed far less harmless, less vulnerable. "He was going to finish out the year and retire. Can you imagine me retired on a horse farm!"

"Trey was going to quit his job?" I couldn't imagine Trey without the bragging rights of a badge.

"He bought the Trainor farm for us. He even put my name on the lease. I told him I was leaving town, but even at the end, I don't think he believed me."

"I didn't know Trey knew anything about horses."

"His silent partner—the one who helped him buy the farm—knew about horses and advised him on how to look for good horse flesh. That's what Trey called it, horse flesh."

"Jenny, this sounds so expensive and a little crazy. How could you go along with it?"

I'd hit a nerve and saw a steely resolve in her eyes. In a split second, her face went from sweet to something way the opposite of sweet. "I don't think that's your business," she said. "I don't ask you how you got that sugar daddy stepfather to set up your trust fund." She practically spit the words at me.

"Jenny!" What a little bitch. "How do you know about the trust fund?"

"This is a very small town full of very big mouths." She was obviously pleased that she had me on the ropes.

"It's none of your business what I have or don't have." I meant to stand straight and create an impression of strength, but when I stepped back to stand taller, I tripped over my own two feet. As I fell toward the ground, I barely missed a rabbit statue that Aggie had given Elli long ago.

"I'd ask you in, but it's way too late. Now be careful," she added. "This is a town where bad things happen almost daily." Slam! The door was closed and Jenny's nasty little face was gone. Talk about being wrong about someone!

She wasn't going to get away that quickly, though. I drove my car around the block and parked. Not the brightest move, I know, but I wanted to see just who Jenny was expecting. I slowly crept into Jenny's yard, aiming toward the backdoor, where no light was on. I'd have a better view of both the side and the rear of the house.

"Hi, Sam." Every nerve in my body came alive. I turned and saw Luke Barrett, no smile.

"I was just at Jenny's, and I think I left my purse," I said. "I'm going back to get it. Are you on your way to the office?" Never give too lengthy an explanation, isn't that the rule? I'd let him figure out why, if I was so innocently on my way back to Jenny's, that he found me crouched behind a tree.

"No office tonight."

That's what I feared. Luke was the second person whom I'd judged far too kindly. "You mean you're here to see Jenny?" *As I spoke the words,* I thought *Oh, my god! Jenny was the woman Luke couldn't get out of his head! Jenny was the one in the car who had chased the four of us that night! And Luke was Trey's silent partner.*

"I can tell by the look on your face, Sam, that unfortunately you've finally added one plus one correctly." Luke was disdainful, even hateful. "Jenny called right after you paid her a visit. She thought you'd hang around and snoop. You're too nosy for your own good. Well, there's no way anyone is going to mess up my plan to give Jenny the life she deserves."

What she deserves, I thought, *is life plus thirty.*

"Walk slowly toward the house, with me," he gave me a not-so-gentle shove. "If you make one bit of noise, I'll crush your throat with my bare hands."

Luke had been the man behind me on the stairs that night. It was Luke's hands shoving my head against the toilet bowl. It was Luke who shot Messy. It was so obvious and yet we'd missed it, all of us.

"Luke, we all tried to help you. How could you be the one who killed so many people?"

"Shut up and get in there." He pushed me through the door.

"I told you she'd stay around to spy. Why did you bring her back here, though? Someone might have seen you walk in." Sweet butter-wouldn't-melt-in-her-mouth Jenny had left and in her place was Lady Macbeth on steroids, a schemer, a manipulator, a murderer. Standing before me, her face full of loathing, was the person who'd orchestrated all the pain, fear, and suffering our town had experienced in the past few grisly weeks.

"Are you sure no one saw you? We can't blow it now." She was practically foaming at the mouth.

"I tried to throw her off the scent, honey, but she was already on to us." He was simpering and slobbering when he talked to Jenny.

"We've got to get out of here now. I wanted to stay a while, but I'll take the money that Trey put in the Swiss bank account and head for South America. I'll leave for Chicago and then catch a plane in a few days."

"You? What about me, darling? I did all those things for you. You told me that Trey was abusing you and that your uncle and Lacy's aunt were threatening you." Luke's condescending behavior made me want to throw up—that and the knowledge that I would very soon be lying in my very own pool of blood.

"Luke, you were the one who nearly choked me to death." I stalled, hoping that Charley, my dad, Lacy—anyone—would surmise I might be nuts enough to have gone to talk to Jenny on my own.

"No, stupid. You stupid bitch!" Jenny pushed me so hard I slammed into the wall. "I was the one who ran you off the road. Trey paid one of his jailhouse buddies to strangle you, but the guy effed it up. Then he tried to rob a bank and they arrested him. Fortunately, very fortunately you might say, for us, somehow he managed to hang himself in his cell."

Another murder to chalk up to Trey and company.

"Why me?" I knew when I stopped talking, I'd stop living.

"Why me?" Jenny mocked me. "Simple. We thought you knew more than you did. Trey and I knew Elli had figured out some things we didn't want her to know, and we also knew she went looking for you. Turns out she didn't have time to tell you anything, but by the time we found out, Burt had already killed Elli. Our bad."

"Burt killed her?"

"Yep. Trey let the dirty scumbag think he was in for some money until Elli spilled the beans about Lacy's father to you. He got so mad he killed her. It wasn't our idea, but it worked to our advantage." Jenny laughed the laugh of a maniac. "And she didn't have time to give you the news about Lacy and Charley being brother and sister. Isn't that funny?"

Elli's big news had killed her.

"So then Trey killed Burt?"

"Wrong. Trey's bank robbing buddy killed him too. Turns out people will do bad things for a couple hundred bucks."

"Honey," Luke was practically on his knees in front of Jenny, "I think you're telling too much." He immediately jumped up and started pacing. Jenny wasn't the only maniac.

"You sure used Trey and Luke to get what you wanted," I said.

She picked a cup off the table and threw it. "What's the matter? Jealous that I've got so many and you can't hold any man? And let me tell you, they both got what they wanted." She brushed up against Luke, and I could see she was his sexual catnip. For a minute, I thought he would grab her and throw her to the floor in front of me. "Not now. We've got to get rid of her." Jenny slithered up and down against him and turned to me.

Luke would have made a great Nazi. "She had a great plan but you had to keep digging deeper and deeper," he snarled at me.

"It was a great plan, wasn't it?" She kissed him nearly biting off his lower lip. "But now we both have to be clever and shut this one up forever."

I bought time. "Jenny, I have to admit, you're quite a mastermind. How did you pull all this off? All along I was sure Trey was the one making the plans."

"He made plans to have me in his bed. And my plan was to get him to do what I wanted." She breathed deeply sending her pointed breasts to direct Luke's attention. He was mesmerized by them and her.

I was full out terrified and trying my damndest not to show it. "Well, when I worked for that old fart Cotter, I heard Trey blackmailing him. I didn't know what it was about, but I knew it meant big bucks because Old Man Cotter had big bucks. That's when I decided to get to know Trey real well. He had a girlfriend, but Lacy was no competition. Men go wild for me, you know."

When Jenny was talking, she wasn't slicing and dicing me.

"Trey told me that Burt told him something one night when he was drunk. It was that when he was in jail with Lacy's dad, Robert Pickett, had confided in him that he had a feeling he wasn't Lacy's real dad. And it pissed him off. He told Trey that when he found out who it was, he'd kill him. Trey started keeping his ears open and noticed that when Cotter was in the restaurant, he was always talking to Mabel in low tones. And when Trey worked in pest extermination—hey, that's kind of what I am now, a pest exterminator—anyway, when he worked getting rid of bugs, he was at Cotter Manufacturing sometimes. When he was there he started listening and paying attention. Trey was no dummy, and pretty soon he'd put two and two together.

He figured if Old Man Cotter could give Mabel bundles of money, then he could give some to Trey too."

"So how did Elli find out?" I asked her.

"Her damn bread. She was delivering it to the factory and heard Trey shaking down Cotter. She told Burt that she was going to get you to put it all in the paper. Burt told Trey and the rest is history." Again, that malevolent laugh.

"That's where I come in," Luke seemed eager to share credit for the despicable deeds. "A few months ago, Jenny came to my agency to look over Burt's insurance. There wasn't much, but she broke down and told me what her father, and a lot of other sick, debauched men, had done to her. She couldn't go to the police because Trey had taken advantage of her when she was young and was still threatening her if she didn't have sex with him when he demanded it."

That's when you fell hook, line, and sinker. Jenny reeled you in. "What about Charley's dad?" *Surely, someone was searching for me by now.*

"Trey hated Charley and his dad," Jenny said. "He hated rich people. He went to Charley's dad and told him he knew about Lacy and about how he used Lacy's mother. Now I don't think he used her, but Mr. Cotter couldn't stand thinking people in town would think that so he pretty much agreed to whatever Trey asked. Trey got a butt load of money from him. I think he had over two million, but a few weeks ago, Mr. Cotter called him and told him that he couldn't take it anymore. We all know how that ended. Trey then went to Mabel, dear old bitch that she was. There was no way she was going to be blackmailed so she told him to get out, or she'd have him arrested. I was the one who took care of that pitiful excuse for a woman. Who was she to act so high and mighty? She'd gotten rich off Cotter and didn't want others to share the wealth. I liked pushing that knife into her. Then Lacy told Mabel had left me some money in her will, and I felt bad for about two seconds." Hideous laughter.

Her smile made me physically ill.

So it was never supposed to be Mabel's money. Charles Cotter had intended it for Lacy from the beginning.

"Trey was putty in my hands, very hard putty. Then he started being nasty, wanting me to do things." She feigned helplessness as she smiled at Luke. "Luke helped me get Trey to put me on his insurance policy and in his will. Then he took care of Trey. Luke's grandmother died of cancer and he had a way of getting hold of her old chemo drugs. They were very effective."

"You are very effective," she said to him before she stuck her tongue in his mouth.

"So," I interrupted Sin-e-max. "Basically, you killed mostly decent people to get rich."

"Can you think of a better reason?" asked Luke.

"Not yet, precious," said Jenny. "First we have to get rid of our little dilemma." She nodded her head in my direction.

"And we need to talk about both of us leaving for Chicago tonight." There was no way Luke was going to get left.

"Oh, I'll go there so no one gets suspicious, and then you'll join me, and we'll fly to South America together."

Luke didn't look convinced. "I can't have you leaving without me." Now he was whining.

Jenny had a one-track mind. "Let's get this over with. Take her into the bedroom."

I was so panic-stricken, my eyes were throwing flares, but I stayed in the game. "I thought you said you were going to Costa Rica. That's in Central America, not South America."

"I said it to throw people off the track. We're a modern-day Bonnie and Clyde."

Bonnie anyway. Clyde looked weak, scared, and horny. I totally sympathized even though I hated him almost as much as I hated her. My skin and hair tingled from considering how they might choose to get rid of me.

"Move!" Luke might be a simpering twit with Jenny but he was a thug with me.

Jenny shoved me onto the bed. "Stay there!" she shouted.

I was lightheaded. Poor Messy! She'd wonder where I was and when I was coming home. I wasn't. I felt I was about to erupt in tears. I wouldn't let that happen. I wouldn't give creepy little Jenny Lundy the satisfaction.

"Tell me you're not going without me." Luke was beyond pathetic with her. Then he slapped duct tape over my mouth and wrapped it around my hands so tightly it burned into my skin.

"You have to trust me," again her hand went to his crotch. "I know what's best for you, don't I?"

Slap the tape over my eyes, I thought. *I don't want to see what's about to happen here.*

"Oh, Jenny," I watched his eyes roll back in his head and closed my own.

"There you go. That's my Luke."

He pushed her to the floor and rolled on top of her. She struggled to get him off. "Not now. Luke, we need to get rid of Sam. But Luke was in a trancelike state, ripping at Jenny's clothes and frantically kissing her. Okay, so I opened my eyes again.

"God, Jenny!" Luke screamed. "What did you do?"

When I opened my eyes again, Luke was on the floor with blood spurting from his chest. Before he could utter another sound, Jenny again plunged a large pair of scissors into his gaping chest. Within seconds, Luke was dead. And I was next.

"You pig!" she stood looking down at him and kicking his lifeless body. "You're just like all men. Your dirty hands all over me as if they owned me. Your smells. Your sounds. I hate you all." Then, horrifyingly, Jenny stopped screaming and looked at me. "And you, you snoopy whore. This would have been so easy if you'd left well enough alone. Trey and me had a great thing going and you screwed it up. Then I had to hook up with that pathetic excuse for a man." Again she kicked Luke's body. "They all wanted to use me. No one uses me," she shouted at the top of her lungs. Next she sat on the floor and pulled her legs to her chest. "I never should have gotten rid of Trey. He took care of me."

She shook her head and wept. "You damn well better write the suicide note I'm going to tell you to write," she stood and pulled me off the bed. "You're going to write how the guilt got to you and how you and Charley were the ones who killed everyone to keep people from knowing about Lacy and about how Charley drove his father to kill himself."

"No one will believe that. You're done, Jenny. You need to give yourself up."

She held the point of the scissors against my right eye. "We can make this very, very slow," she hissed. "I love watching people I hate suffer, and I hate you."

I nodded that I'd do what she wanted. It would buy me a little more time, whatever good that would be.

"Good. I kill people, and I'm good at it. It's made me a rich girl—and it's made me free. I'm free from all those men who want to play grab ass with a little girl.

Dirty men with stupid wives who let them take me down to the basement and put their dirty hands in me and hurt me."

"Burt deserved to die. If no one else died, he needed to die. All those nights when he'd sneak into my bedroom. I hated him!" she screamed into the darkness. "And that preacher and his wife! Don't get me started on them. Both of them couldn't get enough of me."

I could see now what I'd missed before. Jenny Lundy was absolutely, out of her mind, crazy. And maybe she was crazy enough to make her plan work. She *was* the brains behind a series of unsolved murders. We'd all missed it because nothing looks more convincingly sane than a total whacko. One sweet-looking girl had paralyzed a town and made everyone in it afraid of his or her own shadow.

"I'm going to free one of your hands." She was cold and calm. "And you're going to write just what I tell you because if you don't, I'm going to leave here and kill a lot of people you love, even that dog who lived when it should have died."

Oh, no she didn't. She was the one who'd hurt Messy!

She untied my hands, and the second she did so, I grabbed her wrist.

"Don't do that!" she drove the scissors into my arm. The pain was unbearable. "Now you'll have to use the other hand to write the letter."

I felt myself losing consciousness. Never had I felt anything as awful as the blood pulsing from my arm and the ensuing ache. Jenny was going to kill me, but before that I was going to suffer. She'd make sure of it.

"Put that down, Jenny," Scoop's voice was the most wonderful sound I'd ever heard.

"You old drunk," she snarled. "A lot of good you'll do. You're probably the only old fart in this town who hasn't reached into my panties. Want to now?" Jenny walked seductively toward him, pointing the scissors at him. "Get out of my way."

"Put down the scissors." He stood between her and her escape.

"No!" She charged at him and drove the scissors into his shoulder, barely missing his neck. At the same time, he put his leg behind hers and pushed her backwards. She struggled to rise, the scissors tightly gripped in her hand. Scoop kicked her hard in the side so she again fell to the floor, very close to where Luke lay. It was then that Scoop stepped forward, put his big shoe on her neck and pressed down. "This is for Elli," he said as he crushed the life out of Jenny Lundy.

"This is a nice mess you've gotten us into." Scoop surveyed the two bodies as he pulled the tape from my mouth and untied my hands.

"How did you find me?" I struggled for air.

"Trailed you. Been trailing you for days. But I got so tired, I fell asleep and when I got to your house but you weren't there. I called Lacy, and she told me some places where she thought you'd be. Charley wasn't home. Your mother was in bed asleep, and this was third on their list."

Thank god for friends who listen and fathers who spy, I thought.

"I probably should be mad at you for following me, but somehow, all I want to do is hug you." And I did. I couldn't remember when I last hugged Scoop.

"I knew you wouldn't stop sticking your neck out, not my Sam. I also knew you'd eventually get yourself into a jam you couldn't get out of." Then he said something I never thought I'd hear. "I love you very much, you know."

Finally, I said something I never thought I'd near myself say, "I love you too, Dad."

"Now I think we both need the emergency room. Maybe we can get a twofer." Scoop and I helped each other up and waited until the police and ambulance got there. Whether or not I passed out on the way to the hospital is up for debate, but I remember waking up with Charley's great face next to mine and Messy licking my hand.

"Dogs can't be in here." I said.

"They can if your family donated two wings to this place," he picked me up and held me as if he'd never let me go. "We have to stop meeting like this," he said as Aggie, Lacy, my mother, Jersey, and even the very timid Hilda ran in. Charley just kept holding me to him, and it seemed fine with everyone else.

Chapter Twenty

Small towns are great for a lot of reasons, not the least of which is that they're forgetful. By the time spring rolled around, it was as if nothing exciting ever happened in Cotter's Corner. In fact, even though I'm writing a syndicated series based on the murders, it's as if I'm writing about another town. I want to keep it that way because I don't want to immortalize my precious town as a haven for maniacs.

Even now, months after Jenny's death, I walk around in a swirl of emotions. The uppermost is my increasing appreciation and love for Charley who was and continues to be indescribably kind, tender, and understanding since my up close and personal experience with Jenny.

Neither Scoop nor I were seriously injured. Of course, my mother acted like we were both at death's door. She put us in adjoining rooms in her house and waited on us hand and foot. I got up and out as soon as possible, but not Scoop. He stayed until she practically threw him out. Who knows what will happen there. I know that Mother and Scoop are not the people they were when they severed all their ties decades ago. And I wish them well, whatever they decide to do.

Lacy? She had no idea that Charles Cotter, Senior, was her father, but fell in with the idea pretty quickly. "I've always like Charley and now I know it's more than because we're old friends. Won't all those snobby women who didn't want me dating their sons be glad to open their doors to me!"

Because she was already wealthy from what Charley's dad had given Mabel, Lacy fought Charley's determination to split everything with her; so totally behind her back, he did it anyway.

There's no ring from Charley, and we want it that way. I know we're as much in love as any two people can be, but we like taking it slow. We take everything very, very slowly, if you get my drift. I have no doubt the ring will come, but I'm not worried about when.

Aggie is still Aggie. Sewing with me, Hilda, and my mom, and spreading gossip, real or imagined. The latest big news from her is that the bonus Charley gave Wes Falls for his great work was enough to buy Dottie that ring. We're all invited to the wedding because Charley's hosting the reception at his house. "I owe Wes," he said. "If he hadn't come clean with you, we might not have caught on to Jenny. And I couldn't have lived if she had done anything to you."

Jersey has taken loads of work off Charley's shoulders. A month ago, he bought the Trainor farm, which reverted to Charley once the law discovered how Trey had accrued his ill-gotten gains. In the fall, the farm will host a wedding, a small intimate gathering to celebrate the union of Malachi White of Jersey City, New Jersey, and Lacy Pollock Cotter of Cotter's Corner, daughter of Charles Cotter and Sheila Pollock. Maybe Charley and I aren't ready to take the big step but Jersey and Lacy are. "Hey, I've kissed my frogs," she laughed when she showed me the diamond and ruby ring Jersey gave her last week for her birthday. "I know a prince when I see one."

Charley never deposited the check Jersey gave him for the farm. Half of it belonged to Lacy anyway, and the other half is his wedding gift to them.

So what will happen to Lacy's house? The one she lived in with Mabel? That house is her gift to Wes Falls when he marries Dottie. Hilda and Aggie say it's the sweetest thing they ever heard. But they aren't going to be left out. My mother and I have decided that they need to spruce up their houses, and she's going to let them pick out paint, paper, carpeting, and appliances while they stay at her house during the remodeling. If I thought my mother would ever return to being the doyenne of Chicago, I had nothing to fear. Cat Hayes is home forever.

And Leland? The judge and he didn't work out. But he and Thurgood struck up quite a friendship so he gets the little boy every other weekend and two months in the summer. I'm glad for both of them. I know the value of spending summers with your father.

Next week, Charley and I are going to Provo to be with Rosie. She'll love him. And she'll see immediately that I do.

If this story all sounds too good to be true, please don't doubt it and be happy for me. Life isn't always easy. Mine sure wasn't, but look how much better it got because I can't stop snooping.

ABOUT THE AUTHOR

Lyla Fox spent over twenty years teaching English from first grade, to high school, and college. During that time she also wrote everything she could from newsletters, to letters-to-the-editor, to a children's novel which won a Writer's Digest Honorable Mention, and articles for national magazines such as *Newsweek*, *Forbes*, *Parents,* and various other national and regional publications. With her two children grown and living two thousand miles away and a husband devoted to the golf course, Lyla is thrilled to have time to work in the genre that has captivated her since fourth grade when she discovered the adventurous Nancy Drew. *Snoop* is her first mystery, but she's already far into two others with equally trying situations and quirky characters.

www.ingramcontent.com/pod-product-compliance
Lightning Source LLC
Chambersburg PA
CBHW050421260626
47156CB00003B/1109